THE RATS

The Rats

JAMES HERBERT

NEW ENGLISH LIBRARY/TIMES MIRROR

First published in Great Britain by New English Library Ltd., 1974
© James Herbert 1974

First NEL Paperback Edition November 1974
A new edition July 1976
Reprinted September 1976, January 1977
Reissued in this new edition April 1977
Reprinted September 1977
Reprinted November 1977
This new edition June 1978
Reprinted May 1979
Reprinted August 1979
Reprinted February 1980

NEL Books are published by
New English Library Limited from
Barnard's Inn, Holborn,
London, EC1N 2JR
Reproduced, printed and bound in Great Britain by
Cox & Wyman Ltd, Reading

450042774

THE RATS

Prologue

The old house had been empty for more than a year. It stood, detached and faded, next to a disused canal, away from the road, screened by foliage gone wild. No one went there, nobody showed much interest anymore. A few windows had been shattered by the neighbourhood kids, but even they lost interest when nothing more than silence responded to the crash of broken glass. In fact, the only interest that had ever been shown by others was on the day they took the old woman away.

They knew she'd been living alone since her husband had died, never went out, and was only rarely seen peering from behind lace curtains. She never parted the curtains, just gazed through them, so only a hazy, spectral form could be seen by anyone interested enough to look. Her groceries were delivered every week and left on the back step. Powdered milk was included amongst them. The local grocer said the old woman's bank paid her bills regularly every three months with never any queries as to the contents of his delivery. Which suited him. He'd been given a list at the beginning for a regular order, but if he forgot to include a pound of butter or two pounds of sugar now and again, no one noticed – no one complained.

Still, he was curious. He used to see her occasionally when her husband was alive, but even then she didn't have much to say. They were a couple of queer old birds, her and her old man. Never going out, never having company. But well off because they'd been abroad for years and since their return the husband never seemed to work. Then the old boy had died. The grocer wasn't sure of what but it had been a recurrence of some tropical disease he'd caught whilst abroad. The old woman was never seen after that, but the grocer had heard her. Nothing much, just the scraping of chairs or a door closing. He'd once heard her shouting at someone, but never discovered who.

People had begun to wonder about her. Some heard wailing coming from the house one night. Laughter another. Finally, complete silence for over a month.

It was only when the grocer found his previous week's delivery still on the doorstep that he reluctantly reported the matter to the police. Reluctantly, because he feared the worst and hated to see a nice little, regular order come to an end.

Anyway, it turned out she wasn't dead. A policeman was sent to investigate and then an ambulance arrived and took her away. She wasn't dead, just a lunatic. As far as the grocer was concerned she might just as well have passed on because that was the end of his little number. It had been too good to last.

So the house was empty. Nobody came, nobody went, nobody really bothered. In a year it was barely visible from the road. The undergrowth was tall, the bushes thick and the trees hid the upper storey. Eventually, people were hardly aware it existed.

Chapter 1

Henry Guilfoyle was slowly drinking himself to death. He'd started six years ago, at the age of forty. He'd been a successful salesman for a Midland paper company and was ready to become area manager. The trouble was, he'd fallen in love late in life. And unfortunately, he'd fallen for one of his junior salesmen. He'd trained young Francis for five weeks, taking him on his business journeys up and down the country. At first he wasn't sure if the boy had the same inclinations as himself but as he grew to know him, the shyness, and the quiet loneliness of his protegé seemed slowly to dissolve that incredible gap he'd always felt with other men.

Why Francis had decided to become a salesman he'd never discovered. He wasn't the type. Guilfoyle could hold his own in the company of any group of men. He could be the typical bluff salesman; the dirty jokes, the sly wink, the back slapping, the professionalism of his trade hiding any imperfections in his maleness. He was a good actor.

Francis was different. It seemed the shadow of his homosexuality dampened his natural spirits, guilt tainting his moods. But he wanted to prove himself, to be accepted, and he had chosen a career that would make him forget his own personality by reflecting that of others.

The third week they'd stayed in a small hotel in Bradford. Only double rooms were available, so they shared one with single beds. They'd been drinking most of the afternoon with a client, after lunch, taking him to the usual local strip club. Guilfoyle had watched Francis in the darkened basement called a club because it had a bar and a membership fee.

The boy had watched the girls all right, but not with the exaggerated look of lust shown on the face of their client – and on himself, of course. And when the final sequinned garment of the girl had been thrown aside, he slapped the boy's thigh, under the table with skilful heartiness, letting his hand linger, just for a moment, but long enough for their eyes to meet. And then he knew – oh, that glorious moment when he really knew.

There had been signs after the first week of course. Little tests Guilfoyle had set. Nothing daring, nothing that could cause even slight embarrassment if rebuffed. But he'd been right. He knew. He'd seen the smile in the boy's eyes, no surprise, not even apprehension, and certainly not alarm.

The rest of the afternoon passed with a dreamlike quality. His heart beat wildly every time he looked at the boy. But still he acted superbly. His vulgar, and ugly – most definitely ugly – client never suspected. They were men, in a man's world, leering at big breasted, deformed women. The boy was a bit green of course, but they'd shown him how real men acted when they were confronted by naked thighs and fleshy tits. Guilfoyle emptied his glass of Scotch, threw back his head, and laughed.

When they got back to the hotel – the hotel Guilfoyle had chosen for special reasons – the boy was sick. He wasn't used to drink, but Guilfoyle had plied him with whisky all afternoon. Now he began to have regrets. Perhaps he'd overdone it. Francis had been sick in the cab on the way back from the club, and then again in their room, in the sink. Guilfoyle had ordered black coffee and poured three cups into the half-conscious boy. There was a mess on the boy's coat and shirt so Guilfoyle tenderly took them off and scrubbed the worst spots in hot water.

Then Francis began to cry.

He was sitting on his bed, head in his hands, his pale shoulders shuddering convulsively. A lock of fair hair fell over his long, thin fingers. Guilfoyle sat next to him and put his arm over the boy's shoulder. The boy's head leaned into Guilfoyle's chest, and then he was cradling him in his arms.

They stayed like that for a long time, the older man rocking the younger one back and forth like a five-year-old until the sobbing faded into an occasional whimper.

Guilfoyle slowly undressed Francis and put him into the bed. He gazed at him for a while then undressed himself. He got in beside the boy and closed his eyes.

Guilfoyle would never forget that night. They'd made love and the boy had surprised him. He wasn't the innocent he had seemed. Nevertheless, Guilfoyle had fallen in love. He knew the dangers. He'd heard the stories of middle-aged men and young boys, knew their vulnerability. But he was happy. For the first time, after making love to another man, he felt clean. Purged was the feeling of guilt, gone was the feeling of self-contempt, disgust. He felt free – and alive, more alive than he'd ever been.

They'd gone back to their company after collecting a fair-sized order from their client in Bradford, and all had gone well for a while.

Guilfoyle expected to be area manager in a few weeks, large orders were coming in, and he saw Francis every day and most evenings.

Then, slowly at first, things began to change. The younger lads seemed to be losing their respect for him. Nothing much, just a few cheeky back-answers to him. His older colleagues didn't seem to have too much to say to him anymore. They didn't avoid him exactly, but when in his company their conversation was always slightly strained. He put it down to the fact that he was soon to be manager and they didn't know quite how to treat him.

But then he caught some of the typists smirking behind his

back at each other. Old Miss Robson, the office spinster, wouldn't even speak to him.

Finally, that fateful day. It was just after lunch, he'd returned from the local office pub where a table was always reserved for him when he was in town, and had gone into the staff toilet. He went into a cubicle, took his trousers down, sat and began to think about a new business venture he had in mind once he was area manager.

Then he glanced at the back of the door. He froze. It was covered with grafite. All about him. Evidently, after the first one, it had developed into a game, for marks had been awarded to each one. The crude drawings were all of him (he assumed), and Francis, unmistakeably Francis, because of the long hair that fell across his forehead and the gaunt features, cartoon drawings making his love ridiculous. Ugly drawings.

Blood rushed to his head, tears filled his eyes. How could they? How could they destroy their precious love like this? Dirty little minds, coming in here, scratching on the door, sniggering.

He sat there for half an hour, quietly weeping. He finally realised how ridiculous, how pathetic he looked; a middle-aged man in love with a young boy, sitting in a toilet with his trousers round his ankles, crying over words and drawings that understood nothing of his life.

He went home – he couldn't face returning to the office and the smirks of his so-called friends. He drank a bottle of Scotch.

That was the begining of his deterioration. He went back to work next day but now it was different. He was aware. He saw a jibe in every remark made.

He went home again that lunch time, buying a fresh bottle of Scotch on the way.

After two weeks he began to get a grip on himself but suddenly Francis left. He hadn't said goodbye, just left a brief note saying he was sorry but couldn't stand the persecution from the people he worked with any longer.

He went to the boy's home but a hysterical scene with Francis's mother made him realise it was finished. Her threat of involving the law convinced him of this. Francis was very young.

His downhill plunge was rapid after this. He lost his chance of promotion, and was never quite sure if it was because of his reputation or the fact he was rarely sober now. Probably both.

He resigned and moved down to London, to lose himself in the quagmire of countless other disillusioned people. So for six years he hadn't worked much, but had drunk steadily till his money ran out. He was thrown out of lodgings more times than he could remember. He did odd jobs now and then in the markets, mostly Spitalfields, pushing barrows, loading lorries. With the few pence he made from this he bought cheap booze. He slept rough. At one time he'd been able to fulfil his sexual needs in dusty old cinemas, sitting next to men of his own kind. Only twice had he been threatened, once very quietly, with menace, the other time with much shouting and fist-waving, all eyes in the cinema centred on his shame.

But now he was too unkempt for even that. His clothes reeked, his body smelt of grime picked up in the market and the sheds where he slept. Any desire left in his body had been burned out by the cheaply concocted alcohol he now drank.

All he cared for now was saving up his meagre earnings to buy more oblivion.

Guilfoyle had worked hard that week. He'd conquered his craving for drink so that he could buy a complete bottle of cheap gin that Saturday. How he had survived, he never knew, but somehow he'd managed, the mental picture of a full bottle of gin ever-present in his mind. Now, as he shuffled along the dark streets by the docks, he drank until his head spun and his steps became more unsteady.

He climbed through a crumbling window of a house the slum-clearance people hadn't yet cleared. Staggering over rubble, he made his way to the back of the house to be out of the way of any lights shone in by policemen with nothing better to do.

He sat down in the corner of what must have once been the kitchen. Before the bottle was completely empty, he fell into a drunken stupor.

Hours later, Guilfoyle woke with a start. His befogged mind had registered something, but he didn't know what. He'd drained the rest of the gin before he felt the sharp pain in his left hand. As he jerked the hand up to his mouth, he heard something scuttle away. He threw the bottle after the sound when he tasted blood on the back of his hand. It began to throb and the taste of his own sticky blood made him retch.

He rolled onto his side as the gin began to pump from his body and laid there while his body shook.

Suddenly, he felt the pain again in his outstretched left hand. He shrieked when he realised something was gnawing at the tendons. He tried to get to his feet but only stumbled and fell heavily, bruising the side of his face. As he lifted his hand to his face again he felt something warm clinging to it. Something heavy.

He tried to shake it away, but by now it had a firm grip. He pulled at the body with his other hand and felt brittle hair. Through his panic he understood what held him in this monstrous grip. It was a rat. But it was big. Very big. It could have been mistaken for a small dog, but there was no growling, no long legs to kick his body. Only what seemed to be razor-edged claws, frantically beating on his lower arm.

He tried to gain his feet again as he felt more pain in his leg. He screamed.

The blinding pain seemed to run up his leg to his very testicles. More teeth sank into his thigh.

As he stood he felt tiny feet running up the length of his body. He actually felt hot, fetid breath as he looked down to see what could climb a man's body with such speed. Huge teeth that were meant for his throat sank into his cheek and tore away a huge flap.

His body poured blood now as he threshed around. Once he thought he'd found the door, but something heavy leapt up onto his back and pulled him forward onto the floor again.

Rats! His mind screamed the words. Rats eating me alive! God, God help me.

Flesh was ripped away from the back of his neck. He couldn't rise now for the sheer weight of writhing, furry vermin feeding from his body, drinking his blood.

Shivers ran along his spine, to his shocked brain. The dim shadows seemed to float before him, then a redness ran across his vision. It was the redness of unbelievable pain. He couldn't see any more – the rats had already eaten his eyes.

Then, he felt nothing, just a spreading sweetness over his body. He died with no thoughts on his mind, not even of his beloved, almost forgotten, Francis. Just sweetness, not even pain. He was beyond that.

The rats had had their fill of his body, but were still hungry. So they searched. Searched for more food of the same kind.

They had tasted their first human blood.

Chapter 2

Here we go again, thought Harris as he trudged down the dusty road to St. Michaels.

Another bloody week teaching those little sods. Teaching art to little bastards whose best work is on lavatory walls. Jesus Christ!

He felt the same every Monday. The first three lessons in the morning were the worst. Around lunchtime his mood would gradually warm towards his pupils; there were one or two bright sparks amongst that crowd of scruffs. Thomas had brains. Barney had talent, and Keogh – well, Keogh had cunning. He'd never be a banker or an accountant, but he'd make money all right. Maybe not honest money, but he'd do well for himself.

Harris wondered what made one boy stand out amongst others. Keogh wasn't actually clever in academic terms. He didn't look much. Not big built, not slight. But at fourteen he had that cocky self-assurance that made him just that bit different from the rest. Hard up-bringing perhaps. But then, most of the kids in this place had tough home lives. What could you expect when they lived in dockland, fathers either working in factories or in the docks themselves, most of the mothers working as well, so that when the kids got home from school it was to an empty house. Then, when the parents got home, they had no time for them. Still, things were a lot worse in his day. Dockers earned good money these days, so did factory workers. A lot more than he earned as a teacher. The biggest division between working class and middle class nowadays was accent.

He'd come from the same area; the East End had no mystery for him. He remembered when he was at art school, telling some student friends about where he lived. "How colourful", one girl had exclaimed. Colourful! Well, that was one way of describing it. At thirty-two he was back, teaching little facsimiles of his former self. They'd tried to give him a rough time at first, the little bastards, because art, to them, was playtime, and anyone who taught it was queer anyway. But he'd given them the treatment. He'd come down on them so hard, they were scared to whisper in his presence. Sort out the leaders, that was the trick; give them a hard time, show them up.

You didn't have to use their language exactly, but you could use their style. A good sharp clout now and again worked wonders. Because he was young, he had to show he could be a hard nut too. It was pathetic really. The times he'd had to suppress laughter when one of the little villains had tried to stare him out. He'd finally begun to win their respect, so he'd softened up a little, not too much – they'd have taken advantage – but just enough to get them to loosen up a bit.

Keogh was the only enigma. He knew he could get through to the boy, they both knew it – but Keogh would laugh at him with his eyes just at that last moment before mutual understanding was reached, and he'd know he'd lost again.

Harris wondered if it was worth it. He had his choice of schools to teach in but he wanted to help his own kind. No, he wasn't that noble. This was his home ground. He was in his element here. Besides, they paid more for teachers in "underprivileged" areas. Still, Barney showed promise. Maybe if he talked to the boy's parents they'd let him go on to art school . . .

His thoughts were interrupted as he heard the school bell.

Going through the gates he heard the clatter of running foot-steps behind him.

Two giggling girls, both in short skirts, both with bouncing breasts, both about fourteen years old, flounced past.

"Anyway, the crumpet's good." Harris smiled to himself.

He was half-way through the first lesson when Keogh walked in. He wore his usual uniform of short-sleeved, check shirt, braces holding his trousers at half-mast, showing the full length of his heavy boots.

"Good morning, Keogh", said Harris.

"Morning." Arrogant.

"Nice of you to join us."

Silence.

"Well, what's your story this time?" asked Harris. "Trouble with your back? Couldn't get off it?"

A couple of titters from some of the girls made Harris immediately regret his sarcasm. This was no way to break down Keogh's aloofness.

Still silence.

Oh God, Harris thought, he's in a mood. Christ, in my day, the kids were scared of the teachers being in a bad mood. Now, here am I hoping I don't upset *him* too much.

Then he noticed the boy's hand. He had a grubby handker-chief wrapped around it but blood was seeping through.

"Been in a fight?" Harris asked mildly.

"No."

"What then?" Harder.

"I've been bitten," Keogh grudgingly replied.

"By what?"

Keogh looked at his feet, trying to hide the redness creeping over his face.

"By a bloody rat," he said.

Chapter 3

Karen Blakely shrieked with glee as the dog joyfully licked her nose. Only a year old, she was fascinated by this vibrant, four-legged creature who never tired of playing with her -- unless it was time for its food. She grabbed its tail with her pudgy, little hands and pulled with all her tiny might.

The mongrel yelped with obvious relish and leapt around facing the girl again, plying her face with its juicy tongue, causing more delighted giggles and shrieks.

"Shane!" Karen's mother shouted at the excited dog as she came into the room. "You mustn't lick the baby. How many more times must I tell you?"

The dog looked sheepishly at Karen's mother, tongue hanging out, panting with exhilaration. When it saw its water-bowl being filled at the sink it trotted over and began to lap furiously.

"Now, Karen, we'll just have a nice cup of tea and then we'll go out and get the shopping", Paula Blakely said, smiling at her daughter, who was now pulling at the dog's leg. The dog and the little girl had both arrived about the same time; Karen prematurely, Shane as a present from Paula's husband,

Mike. It was supposed to keep her occupied while waiting for the birth of their first child, but on the same day she'd gone into labour and had been rushed off to the hospital. It had taken twelve hours though for the baby to emerge, and the pain had been enough to discourage her from wanting any more. But she loved that child, more, she thought, than she loved Mike. Maybe because she was the only thing that really belonged to her. Perhaps not quite that. It was more because Karen was something she had produced, she had introduced into the world.

Looking at the gleeful baby, Paula smiled. Or was it just that she was so loveable? Paula and Mike hadn't wanted Karen so soon, they couldn't really afford her. They'd been lucky to get a place so quickly, dingy though it was. It was in a bad area, too near the docks, but they'd lived in Poplar most of their lives anyway, so it didn't make much difference. And it certainly wasn't a slum! Paula made sure of that. Other houses in the street may have been neglected by their tenants, but hers was spotless. Soon, when they'd saved enough money, they'd move out to Barking or Ilford, not too far from Mike's job at the garage, he was doing too well there to leave, but to a better class area, where you didn't have to keep a dog or a cat just to keep the mice down.

The whistle on the kettle began to shrill, interrupting her reverie. She turned it off and reached into the cupboard for the tea tin. She swore when she found it was empty. Mike drank coffee in the mornings but she had never liked its slightly bitter taste. She'd been reared on cups of tea as a child, the teapot in her house rarely being cold.

She looked at Karen for a moment. Would she be all right for a few seconds while she popped next door and borrowed some tea? Yes, she was preoccupied with Shane, watching him now slurp from his food bowl. She wouldn't be long, the baby couldn't get in too much mischief in the few seconds it would take her.

Taking a cup from the cupboard, she quickly slipped out of the room, leaving the door open, hoping Karen wouldn't even notice she was gone.

The baby happily watched the little mongrel gobble his

food. She even tried some on the end of her finger, but spat it out when she discovered it wasn't to her taste.

Suddenly, the dog froze. The hairs on its back stood on end. It snarled at something moving in the doorway. The cellar door, which was in the hall next to the kitchen door, was slightly ajar, and a black shape scurried from it.

Shane bounded towards it, picked it up by its neck and shook it vigorously. A high-pitched squeal broke from the rat. Instantly, another appeared and leapt at the dog's throat, sinking its razor-sharp incisors deep. The infuriated dog spun around in a circle, trying to shake it off but still not letting the first rat go. Then another was on the dog's back, clutching with its claw-like feet, biting hard and ripping skin. Shane howled with pain and shock as more black creatures poured into the room.

The baby began to cry with horror as she saw her beloved playmate being hurt by the foul-smelling creatures.

More rats came into the small kitchen but these were different. These were bigger, moving more cautiously, ignoring the violent struggle with the dog. They saw the crying baby, the bowl of dog food by her side. They slid forward, sniffing the air as they went. The food disappeared rapidly. They turned to the tiny figure.

The dying dog seemed to sense the child's danger, and jumped away from its attackers, three rodents still clinging to its body. It fell upon one huge rat which was already biting into the baby's leg. Shane threw the monster high into the air with its last remaining strength and turned to face the others. The little dog lasted a few seconds more, fighting with frenzied desperation, and then its body was torn to pieces under a black, writhing mass.

When Paula Blakely rushed into the room, she screamed in horror and utter panic. The scene didn't quite register in her brain. All she saw was a room teeming with bestial, furry shapes, tearing at something bloody. And then a small white shape. A tiny hand quivering above the mass of black.

"Karen" she screamed.

She ran into the room, kicking, screaming, her blind panic giving her added strength and speed. She clutched at the arm

and pulled. The little body came up but with two of the monsters clinging. Paula beat at them as she made for the door,
her own legs already covered in blood from the bites she'd
received. The two rats fell away, not from the blows, but because the soft flesh of the child separated from her body.

Paula ran from the house with her dead baby, screaming,
holding the bloody body to her breast.

The rats finished eating the dog, then scurried back into the
cellar, the larger ones first.

Chapter 4

Harris took Keogh to the London Hospital to have the boy's hand seen to. He needed a chance like this to get on more friendly terms with his pupil, and as he had a free period for the next hour, he decided to take the boy himself. Already, on the way to the hospital he seemed more relaxed towards the teacher. When they got there, they were told to wait in the busy casualty department.

"Well, Keogh, how did it happen?" asked Harris.

"I was late, so I took the short cut by the canal," Keogh replied.

"Yes, I know it," Harris said.

The boy raised his eyebrows, but went on. "It was just under the bridge, you know, where the old lock-keeper's house is. Well, there was a dead cat, see, and these two rats dragging it along. Christ, you should have seen the size of them, Mr. Harris. Looked as big as the cat itself. Anyway, they weren't eating it, just sort of dragging it along, you know. So I slung a brick at them." He paused, studying his bloody handkerchief. "Well, instead of running off, they just turned and looked at me. I'd hit one, but he didn't seem bothered. Then, fuck me — oh, sorry, they came at me. So I ran, didn't I. Not before one

had taken a bite out of me hand, though. I kicked him into
the canal and jumped over the wall and ran. But the funny
thing is, when I looked back, there's this other rat, sitting on
the top of the wall, watching me. He must have run right up
after me. Anyway, I didn't hang around, I cleared out."

Harris smiled at the thought of rats big as a cat. Probably
it had been a kitten anyway, and Keogh's nimble mind had
done the rest. But that canal wall was high, he remembered it
from when he was a kid, and even Keogh would have a job
getting over it. But a rat? He knew some could climb, some
species were arboreal, but to scale a six foot high brick wall?
That took some doing.

Just then, all eyes in the casualty department turned as a
hysterical woman, clutching a bloody bundle, was half carried
in by two ambulance men. A nurse dashed forward and tried
to take the small shape from her, but she held onto it fiercely,
her sobs racking her whole body.

It was then that Harris realised what she was holding. It
was a baby. But by the look of its blood-soaked body, it
couldn't possibly still be alive. Oh, the poor little sod, thought
Harris. A doctor came along and tried to soothe the distraught
woman, speaking quietly and calmly, making no attempt to
relieve her of her burden. Then, with his arm around her, and
the nurse on the other side, he led her away.

Everyone in the room appeared shaken by the drama. There
was silence for a few seconds then everyone began to talk at
once, although their voices were hushed. Harris turned to
Keogh whose face was drained of blood and his knees trembled visibly.

Not as tough as you pretend, thought Harris, but he said
nothing to the boy.

It was a while before they got in to see the doctor, who was
very young, much younger than Harris. When doctors and
policemen look like boys, old age *must* be creeping in, mused
Harris.

"Right, lets have a look," the doctor said, beginning to un-
wind the makeshift bandage from Keogh's hand. "Nasty," he
examined the large teethmarks. "What did it?"

"Rat," answered Harris, for Keogh.

"More rats?" The doctor began to clean the wound, causing Keogh to flinch involuntarily.

"What do you mean?" asked Harris.

"Oh, that woman brought in earlier. Her baby had been attacked by rats. Dreadful state." The doctor dabbed ointment onto the wound and began to bandage the hand. "Dead of course, had no chance really. The woman's in a state of shock, blames herself for the whole thing. We had to put her out just to treat her own wounds."

Harris found it hard to speak for a few moments. Anything nasty happening to kids always affected him this way; he'd seen too many of them mistreated to be unaffected by their misfortunes.

He said, "But surely it's unusual for a rat to attack a human being? I mean, I know they can attack very small babies, and even fully-grown men when cornered, but this is different. When they chased the boy here, they could have got away. But they didn't choose to. They attacked instead."

"Yes, I know," said the doctor, taking a syringe from a tray. "Just a quick jab now and you're done," he smiled at Keogh. "But as I understand it from the ambulance men they killed the family's dog to get at the child. Tore it to shreds according to the neighbours who went in afterwards. There was no sign of them though, just a few half-eaten carcasses, presumably killed by the dog, and gnawed at by their canibalistic chums. The cellar door was half open, but nobody ventured down there. That's a job for the police, I suppose."

He placed the syringe in a jar. "There we are. Come back tomorrow and we'll see how it's getting on, all right?" He turned to Harris. "The whole business is very strange. We've always had a few cases of rat bites and even some diseases from them, this being that sort of area, but nothing like this. It's quite incredible. Let's hope they're just isolated incidents and nothing more."

As they left the hospital, Harris noticed Keogh was still trembling.

"What's the matter. Did it shake you up?" he asked kindly.

"Nah, it wasn't that. I just don't feel so good that's all." Keogh wiped his good hand across his brow.

Skiving? wondered Harris. No, he did seem a bit white, and he couldn't fake the perspiration on his forehead. Perhaps it was the after-effects of the injection.

"Okay, you run along home, and take the day off tomorrow if you still feel the same. But make sure you go back to the hospital to get your hand looked at." Harris knew he wouldn't see Keogh tomorrow now, he'd never miss the opportunity of a day away from school. Ah well, he'd been the same as a boy. A chance for a day off couldn't be ignored.

"Cheers," said Keogh, and disappeared around a corner.

On the way back to the school, Harris thought about the rat incidents and the possible implications. He'd seen plenty of the disgusting creatures when he was a boy. He remembered the time years ago when he and his family had sat down to the Sunday lunch and their cat had appeared at the open window, carrying a dead rat in its jaws. They'd laughed at the idea of the cat bringing home its own Sunday lunch as they all jumped up and shooed it away. Another time, one of the neighbours had claimed she was chased down the street by a rat. Her husband had come out with a poker and had run after it, but it had disappeared into one of the bombed houses.

Harris thought they were a thing of the past now, which showed how out of touch you could get living in the top flat of a house in Kings Cross. He supposed they existed just as much, but sanitation experts had driven them literally right underground. Lots of companies had sprung up and made quite a profit out of their extermination. Still, he supposed there wasn't too much to it, it was just that both incidents had happened on the same day. This wasn't the 14th century!

Chapter 5

The old warriors used to gather every night on one of the few remaining bomb-sites left in the East End of London. It was an old churchyard, just off the busy main road of White-chapel and quite near Aldgate East underground station. It was thick with shrubbery and littered with open tombs. A single tower was the only remains of the once majestic church. That night six of them had gathered, safe in the knowledge that they couldn't be seen from the road. All were slowly destroying their insides by their incessant drinking of methy-lated spirits. All had reached the depths of despair, had given up the will to exist with the rest of the world. They rarely spoke to one another, their tormented minds were too occu-pied with their own misfortunes to concern themselves with anybody else's.

Among them was a woman, although barely discernible from the men in their shapeless rags. Mary Kelly was forty-nine, but she looked twenty years older. She cursed the others, cursed herself and most of all, she cursed God. The same God she had worshipped half her life in Ireland. As a child, she'd often gone to Mass three times on a Sunday and once every

day of the week. She'd even gone into a convent at fifteen, but
the solemn, solitary life had not suited her vivacious, although
very religious, personality. Returning to her home town of
Longford, she soon found life too dull for her natural exuber-
ance. Her priest had tried to dissuade her from leaving, but
one day, in the confessional, she'd told him something that
had made him wonder if it wouldn't be best for her to go.
Best for the boys in the town anyway.

The old priest wondered how any child so deeply religious
could have developed such a sinful lust for sex. He finally
decided he'd have more chance of saving her wayward soul if
she remained in the town under his surveillance, so he visited
her parents and persuaded them to make her stay. They had
six other younger children to support, so at first they weren't
too eager to retain this extra mouth, but of course the parish
priest had great influence over his flock. However, the following Saturday, Mary confessed an even greater sin, this time
concerning his young, newly-appointed priest.

She left the following Monday to the relief of the old Father, whose ageing mind could no longer cope with the com-
plexities of this promiscuous saint. Young father Aloysius had
denied the whole affair on being directly, and rather gruffly
questioned, and the old priest had been left in an even more
confused state of mind. Surely, a girl so young and obviously
devout could never make up such lies? But then again, if she
were so devout to God as her record had shown, how could
she be so incited by the evils of the flesh? His only answer was
to pray for her soul and offer up a Mass to save her from eter-
nal damnation.

Mary went to Dublin and got a job as a barmaid in a bar
just off O'Connell street. She met many men of course in her
working hours and resisted none that made advances towards
her.

After a while, not because of her growing reputation, but
because the landlord's wife had discovered her and the landlord himself behind the barrels in the cellar, she had been dismissed. She next found employment in the canteen of a local
brewery where the men soon found she was easy game. The
only thing that puzzled them and caused much joking amongst

them was the fact that she insisted on saying three Hail Mary's
before climbing into bed with them. On her knees beside the
bed, eyes closed, hands clasped tightly together like a child.
They would have laughed even more if they'd known the reason for the prayers.

The first Hail Mary was to ask that she wouldn't fall preg-
nant, the second that she wouldn't get "poxed", and the third
that she would have an orgasm. She'd only learned about or-
gasms from her friends at the canteen and realized something
had been missing all these years. Her craving for sex had never
been satisfied and without knowing why, she had always
sought more and more. It had always been enjoyable, but now
she knew it could be glorious she was determined to experience it. She still attended Mass every Sunday and received
Holy Communion every first Friday of the month. Soon, she
began to go to church two or three evenings a week, to say
the Rosary for the attainment of her sexual goal. It never once
occurred to her that there was anything wrong in this. God
had meant people to enjoy sex, otherwise he wouldn't have
given them this wonderful gift. Hadn't she, as a child, watched
her parents making love so many times without their knowing she was wide awake in the dark of their only bedroom,
listening to their happy sighs and her mother crying out for
Jesus Christ before the final lapse into silence followed by
heavy contented snores.

The regular visits to the church soon came to the attention
of the priest, Father Mahar, who enlisted her aid in the various jobs done by women around God's house. She enjoyed
changing the flowers and dusting the altar pieces and holy
statues, hoping the small sacrifice of her time would not go
unnoticed by God.

She began to help in jumble sales, she visited the old and
the sick, she even joined the choir. Father Mahar was more
than impressed by his new parishioner and began to make
enquiries about her. He learnt that she worked at the brewery
where several of his young male churchgoers were also em-
ployed. When he asked them about Mary he was surprised
by their smirks and guarded answers. Then, one day, a Mrs.
Malone came to see him. He knew her and her husband by

sight, they were regular church-goers, but he hadn't actually spoken to them. They were both young, about thirty-fivish, and seemed good, hard-working people. But on this wet Tuesday morning, Mrs. Malone wore a worried expression, giving her otherwise attractive face hard lines that all too soon would be permanent anyway.

"Ah, it's Mrs. . . . ?"

"Malone, Father."

"Yes, Mrs. Malone. Is there something I can do for you?" The priest's voice was soft, gentle because he could always sense the approaching hysteria in the women who came to see him outside church-going hours.

Margaret Malone's voice trembled slightly as she answered. "It's me Tom, Father. He's . . ." Suddenly, the floodgates were open. She searched in her handbag for a handkerchief.

So soon, thought the priest. How long had this been building up for her to break down so soon in front of me? They could usually get half the story out before the deluge of tears interrupted. He sighed in resignation. He'd heard it so many times before. Tom was being unfaithful or had lost interest in her body, or had taken to beating her every Friday night after a few jars in the pub. How could he comfort these poor creatures, make them realise all things pass, that praying to God at least helped them to withstand the trials of this life.

"Come, now, Mrs. Malone. Let's sit and you can tell me in your own time." He took her arm and led her to a pew at the back of the church. An old woman, wearing a black shawl over her thin, hunched shoulders, lighting yet another candle for the soul of her wayward husband, dead these last six years, paid them no heed. Hadn't she seen it so often before? Hadn't she sat in the same pew, with a different priest so many years ago, pouring out her troubles to her understanding, yet wholly impotent priest?

Margaret Malone at last managed to control her shaking body. "Oh, Father, it's me Tom, he's found another woman."

Father Mahar patted her shoulder and sighed as he waited for the tears to stop again.

"It's a woman at the brewery, Father," she finally went on, her long red hair now damp with her own tears. "It's been going on for weeks. Every Tuesdays and Thursdays he sees her. He said he went to the pub at first, but Deirdre Finnegan told me she'd seen them together, lots of times. And when I asked him about it, he just laughed and said at least she was a better ..." She stopped, remembering she was talking to a priest.

"But he doesn't care, Father. That's what hurts. He doesn't care that I know. He doesn't care about the children. He's obsessed with her. I don't know what to do, Father. What can I do?"

"Now first you mustn't upset yourself, Mrs. Malone," the priest tried to console. "Most men go through this sort of phase at some time or other. It doesn't really mean anything. You'll see, he'll come back to you, and it will be as strong as before. Have courage."

He paused. Now he must be practical. "Do you know the other woman's name? Maybe I can speak to her."

He wasn't quite sure he heard the name correctly through the sobs. It sounded like Mary Kelly.

Father Mahar was stunned. It was Saturday evening, the hour for confession was over, and now he sat alone in his sacristy. Mary Kelly had come to her weekly confession and when she'd finished relating her usual short list of venial sins, he'd asked her about Tom Malone. She hadn't even tried to deny it but spoke quite openly about their affair and when he asked the reason she hadn't confessed it before she asked why she should have to. There was nothing wrong in it, was there?

The priest couldn't believe his ears. The poor child really didn't know there was any sin involved, that what she had done was quite innocent. It was when he questioned her further that he began to doubt her sanity.

She told him of all her other affairs, why she attended church so regularly, and why she prayed so fervently.

All as though it were the most natural thing in the world. And when she asked if it would be possible for him to say a special Mass that she might achieve this wonderful orgasm she'd heard about, he was too shocked to make any reply at all.

He needed time to think, so he asked her to leave but to return in the morning before services. What could he do? She obviously needed medical help as well as spiritual, but how could a doctor cure a girl who was so completely amoral, and how could a priest cure a girl who could not comprehend the difference between right and wrong?

He prayed most of that night, prayed for guidance that he might save this young innocent from her literally soul-destroying fate. The next morning he patiently tried to explain to her why the things she did, and the things she prayed for, were wrong. Not wrong if she found one man whom she could love and eventually marry, make love to achieve a sanctifying union and have children, but wrong if she were to give her precious body to any man who wanted it, just to satisfy this greedy lust within her, and so destroying the spirit of the Holy Ghost who dwelt inside her. God loved her and wanted her to be happy, but she must respect this wonderful gift he had given her, and keep it only for marriage.

She laughed, not out of defiance, but because she genuinely thought the priest was being silly. Her brain had put up a mental block that refused to accept sex as wrong in any way. Where once she had listened to his every word with reverence, she now treated him as though he were the child, and he couldn't be serious in what he was saying.

He went on, explaining about the diseases she could con-tract, the homes she would break up, how it could only lead to unhappiness for herself – but it was hopeless. It wasn't like talking to another person for she was still the sweet, pure young girl he'd come to know – it was as though one section of her brain had closed a door and refused to let any argument enter.

Eventually, he had to suggest that she should see a doctor with him, a good friend of his, who would just talk to her, and between them they would help her back onto the right path. She agreed, although she thought it a silly idea, but if it would please him, then she'd go along. An appointment was made for the following Wednesday, but Father Mahar never saw Mary Kelly again.

Mary moved to another part of Dublin and went back to being a barmaid, her life going on in the same pattern as before. She found a new church to attend but this time she was more wary about becoming too familiar to the priest.

And then, she finally met the man who could fulfil her needs, and, surprisingly enough, she met him in church. Timothy Patrick was an immense man in every way. He had the usual Irishman's ruddy glow, wiry, fair hair, huge hands and ears that stood at right angles from his head. His appetite, not just for food, but for life, was as enormous as his bulk. He was also a good man, not piously religious, but honest and reliable.

As soon as they laid eyes on one another, when he was taking the collection plate round during Mass, instinct told them that here at last was someone who could match their own vitality. He waited for her outside the church, as she knew he would, and walked her to her lodging house. They saw each other every evening after that and on the seventh he took her to a hotel and they made love.

For him, it was the most deeply satisfying act of love he'd ever experienced; for her, it was all her prayers answered. He had laughed when she prayed beside the bed before they made love, but was moved when afterwards she said a complete Rosary in gratitude, understanding this was in some way a compliment to him.

When Mary first saw his size, she was frightened, but she also felt a tingle of excitement run through her. It was in exact proportion to his personality. Enormous. At first he was gentle, more gentle than any other man she had been with, but at her urging, he had become wild, thrusting himself into her with tremendous force, his great hands never still, crushing her breasts, shoulders and thighs. And she fought back with all her might, never allowing him to be dominant, biting, clawing, until she cried for relief from her frenzy. And then relief came, flooding her whole body, making her taut limbs liquid. She wept as he soothed her brow with tender fingers, smiling, talking, staying inside her.

It was then she'd said her Rosary while he waited quietly, his eyes never leaving her bowed head. As soon as she had finished she had laughed and leapt straight back onto the bed, where they made love many more times that night.

They saw each other every day, making love whenever they were alone, their mutual desire never diminishing, always demanding. Finally, Timothy announced his intention to go to England to find better-paid employment and he asked Mary to go with him.

Marriage wasn't mentioned but she eagerly agreed to go and within three weeks they were living together in North London. He found work on a building site and she went back to work as a barmaid. Her faith in God was stronger than it had ever been and she thanked him constantly, in church, at home or even on the bus on her way to work. She cherished her new found love and knew no other man would ever be able to fulfil her the way Timothy did, but she never once tried to push him into marriage.

When war broke out, he enlisted in the army despite her protests. Although she was really proud of him and his action, she dreaded their being apart, for although she knew no other man could satiate her as he did, and no other man could love her as he did, she wondered if she would be strong enough to resist seeking sexual satisfaction elsewhere. Timothy left and within four days she received a letter from him asking her to marry him as soon as he got leave. Then she knew she could wait.

But Timothy died three weeks later, crushed by a tank one night while out on maneouvres. Nobody knew how it had happened; they had just found his body the next morning, the whole of his magnificent torso squashed flat in a field half a mile away from his unit. Nobody knew how he got there or why he was there, but he'd gone on record as being one of the army's first war casualties. Weeks later, one of his friends from basic training had come to see Mary and told her that Timothy had smuggled a flask of whiskey out with him to "keep out the terrible cold" and had wandered off on his own that night. The soldier thought the army had found the smashed bottle with the body and had tried to cover up the matter for both Timothy's sake and the army's.

It was then that Mary had lost faith in God. To give her so much and then to obliterate it with one cruel stroke was too much for her simple mind to take. She began to hate God

almost as much as she had once loved him. They caught her
on her third attempt to burn down a Catholic church. She
was put into an asylum but released after two months as a
model patient. On her second day of freedom she had cost a
priest the hearing on his left side when she'd thrust a knife
into his ear through the wooden mesh-work of a confessional.
She was declared insane and sent back to the asylum. The war
was over by the time she was released and she came back into
a world that was too busy licking its own wounds to worry
about hers.

Her decline was inevitable. She still craved for satisfaction
and sought it in the only way possible, but this time she did it
as a living. She began to drink heavily and soon the many men
began to bore her. None could live up to her Timothy. She
began to mock her clients in their futile attempts to arouse
her, and laughed at their pathetic little organs. One night, a
burly man, proud of his manhood broke her nose when she
derided him. She began losing money, for some men refused
to pay her after her demoralising sarcasm, but still she could
not refrain from her derisive comments on their performance
in bed. She became known to the police as a harasser of
priests; she would follow a priest for miles, either cursing him
or offering him her body, until the poor man had no alterna-
tive but to go into the nearest police station.

She was put away again and again but she always behaved
like a model patient and was soon released. She finally con-
tracted gonorrhoea, and in the early stages, when she knew she
had it, she took great delight in passing it on to the men she
slept with. She soon found herself out on the street when her
landlord fell victim to her ridicule *and* her disease. Her looks
had faded, her appearance was shabby, her mind failed to
grasp reality any more. She went to live with a group of Paki-
stani immigrants in Brick Lane and stayed there for several
years, being used by all the men either collectively or singly,
but eventually they tired of her and threw her out. She went
back one night, months later, and poured paraffin through
the grating into the basement of their dilapidated house, set
a whole box of matches alight and threw it in. One fireman
and five of the Pakistanis died in the fire that burnt the house

to the ground, but nobody suspected Mary of having caused it.

She was found one day, half-dead, on a bomb-site. It took months of hospital treatment to cure her of all her ailments and where the doctors left off the Salvation Army took over. They found her a place to live, bought her new clothes and got her a job in a laundry – they felt sure they could save her from herself.

And they almost did. She worked hard, her maltreated body began to regain some of its former vigour, her mind closed another door, this time to memories. But as she grew healthier, so her body began to demand gratification. Unfortunately, the only personal contact she had with men now was the Salvation Army officer who visited her twice a week at her basement flat. When she tried to seduce him he made the mistake of calling her to look to God. Suddenly, she thought of the joy that had been snatched away by Him after all her devotion to His church. When she'd found her reward, her Timothy, He had taken it away. even his servants, the priests, had tried to prevent her from finding this happiness, and now this other man of God, this so-called "soldier" of God was trying to deny her, hiding behind *Him*, using *His* name, reminding her of *His* treachery.

The Salvation Army officer fled when her hysterical ravings grew into physical violence. Mary left the flat and roamed the streets offering her body to every man she came across, abusing and cursing them as they refused, some jeering, most frightened by her lunatic ranting. She finally had to find her solace in a bottle of Johnny Walker, bought with her meagre savings from her job in the laundry.

That night an ambulance was called to a public convenience at the Angel, Islington, where the attendant had found a woman lying unconscious in one of the cubicles. She had thought the woman was just drunk at first, the smell of alcohol was overpowering, but then she'd noticed the blood seeping from between the woman's legs. It took a doctor two hours to remove all the fragments of glass from Mary's vagina. She'd sought consolation from the whiskey bottle in more than one way.

Mary Kelly looked around at her five companions. Her rav-
aged face contorted with contempt for them. Dirty, dried-up
old men. Not one of them a real man. Not one would pass
their bottle around. Well, tonight she had her own bottle, and
it wasn't meths. It was good Scotch. It had only taken three
days to get enough money to buy the half-bottle. And it had
been easy money to get for she'd gone to the West End, to
the cinema and theatre queues and just stood in front of
people, staring at their faces, one hand outstretched ready to
receive money, the other hand scratching. Scratching her hair,
her arm-pits, her breasts – it was when her hand began travelling towards her crotch that they usually coughed up.

So here she was amongst the grave-stones and the rubble
of the bombed church. It had taken years of wretchedness,
torments to both mind and body to bring her to this point.
But she was amongst her own kind, crushed by life itself. She
unscrewed the top and raised the bottle to her lips with a
wavering hand.

"What's that you're drinking, Mary?" came a voice from
the darkness.

"Fuck off." Mary knew this would happen, that the others
would see her booze and beg for some, just a little drop, one
swig, but she couldn't resist the impulse to come here tonight
and gloat; to make men plead with her. She knew that they'd
even make love to her for just a drop then she could mock
them even more. The old men would forget her filth and she'd
forget theirs, and they'd desperately try to get a hard-on with
their ridiculously wasted pricks so they could fuck her and
earn their drink. But they'd never managed it, and she would
just laugh and enjoy the misery on their loathesome faces.

"Ah, come on, Mary, what's that you're drinking?" A figure
crawled forward towards her.

"None of your business, scum," Mary said, her voice still
heavy with Irish, after so many years.

Other heads lifted themselves from their stupor and turned
towards her. The figure came nearer. Two rheumy, yellow
eyes gazed at the bottle she now held with two hands.

"Come on, Mary, it's me – Myer." The eyes took on a crafty
look as they realised it was nearly a full bottle of Scotch. "I

know what you like, Mary, gimme a drop, and I'll do it for you."

"You," Mary jeered. "You, I remember last time. You couldn't even find it, could you?" Mary began to giggle, her shoulders jerking with the effort. "You!"

The old man began to snigger, too. "That's right, Mary, but it'll be different this time, you see." Grimy fingers began to fumble at his trousers.

Mary laughed now, rocking backwards and forwards, drinking freely from the bottle.

"Just a minute, Mary, I'll soon have it." Myer was laughing, stopping now and then as a concentrated frown swept over his face. "Don't drink it all, Mary." His puzzled look turned into a smile of triumph as he finally produced the object of his search.

Mary's laughter reached a hysterical pitch as she pointed at his limp penis.

"You couldn't fuck a polo mint with that, you daft old sod," she cried.

Just then, a hand grabbed at the neck of the bottle.

"Give us that, bitch," a man loomed over her, his face almost hidden behind wild, curly hair and beard. But the hand had no strength and Mary was invigorated with the Scotch and the laughter. She pulled it back, crouching over it, clutching it between her thighs. The bearded man struck weakly at the back of her neck, but Mary laughed even more.

Old Myer tried to grope between her knees to reach the bottle but she clasped it tightly. "Just one, Mary, just one," he pleaded.

The other man suddenly kicked her, then grabbed her matted hair, pulling her head back, screaming obscenities. She struck out with one hand knocking him onto his back, but Myer made a lunge at the bottle. He doubled up in pain as a bony knee hit his groin.

The three other old warriors crouched and watched, slowly edging forward, eyes never leaving the bottle. The bearded man struggled to his feet and came staggering towards her, like a degenerated bull in rage, but she clawed at his eyes,

drawing blood, sending him to his knees. She turned to face
the other three and they drew back in fear.

"Bastards!" she shouted at them. She turned her back on
all of them, Myer on all fours, tears streaming from his eyes,
still pleading, the bearded man rubbing at his eyes, the three
on the ground cringing. She sucked noisely at the bottle, then
grabbed at her skirt, missed and grabbed again, hoisted it to
her waist, and waved her bare arse at their faces. Then she
disappeared into the bushes and all they could hear was her
mocking laughter.

She stopped by an old tomb, still giggling and muttering to
herself. Men, she thought, all the same. All weak, every one
of them. She'd enjoyed herself tonight, she'd made fools of
them all. She thought of Myer and his tiny prick, like a little
white worm in the moonlight. Pathetic. She'd never known
any man who – no, there had been someone. Now who had
that been? Years ago . . . she drank from the bottle and tried
to recollect who it was that she'd once loved, who was it that
had once given her something? But what? What had she been
given? She couldn't remember.

The rock struck her exposed throat as her head tilted far
back to drink from the bottle. She fell forward and the bearded tramp pulled it from her grasp. He drank deeply, while the
others kicked the moaning form on the ground. Myer took
the bottle next and greedily gulped at the fiery liquid only
releasing it to another when the burning in his throat caused
him to splutter and choke. The man with the hairy face swayed
from side to side and looked at Mary's writhing body. He
knew this bitch, seen her laughing at his friends before, even
laughed at *him* once when he'd tried to do her a favour. He
picked up a large brick and brought it down hard on her
face.

He grabbed the bottle off a thin little man who'd only just
got it into his possession, and drank. They all sat round in a
circle, only a few feet from Mary's still body, finished off the
Scotch and then returned to their meths.

Mary Kelly wasn't quite dead, but she was close to it. Her
skull had been fractured by the brick, and was bleeding pro-

fusely. Two ribs were broken and her throat had a deep gash in it. She had lain in the dirt for a long while, her life-spirit slowly ebbing away, and in a short while she would be dead. All that moved were her lips which seemed to be saying some soundless prayer, over and over again, and her fingers that tried to count to ten endlessly.

Quite nearby lay the slumped bodies of her five companions, huddled together in disturbed slumber.

The first rat approached her cautiously, the smell of blood overcoming any fear, but never blurring its cunning. It was much larger than the other rats that followed it, and darker in colour. When it was a few feet away from Mary it stopped, its hind quarters bunching up, its whole body tensed and quivering.

Suddenly it leapt at the open wound in her throat, sinking its huge incisors deep and drawing out the blood with violent spasms of its powerful body. Mary tried to stir, but she was too weak from blood already lost, the rat now biting deep into her vocal chords. Her body shook, but suddenly another furry form buried half its head into the matted hair over the wound in her skull. Her back arched as her nerve-ends tautened and she fell forward again. Another rat pulled at her ear. Suddenly, her whole body was covered, teeming with squealing creatures as more scurried from the darkness, the smell of blood much stronger than it had been before. So Mary Kelly's unfortunate life ended. The priests had never managed to save her soul, but then it had never really been lost. Only her mind.

The rats drained her body of blood and gnawed her flesh until not much more than bones and pieces of skin remained. It didn't take long, for there were many of them. So many, that not all had been fully-gorged. Their hunger for human flesh had been merely inflamed – they wanted more. There were several larger rats amongst them now, and those began to move towards the five human shapes sleeping nearby.

There was no caution now as they swarmed over the bodies. Two men had no chance, for their eyes were torn from their heads as they slept. They crawled blindly around amidst the carnage that was taking place, rats clinging to their bloody flesh.

The bearded man had risen to his feet, pulling a wriggling body from his face and tearing mostly hair from his cheek in the process. But as he stood, one of the larger rats leapt at his groin, pulling away his genitals with one mighty twist of its body. The tramp screamed and fell to his knees, thrusting his hands between his legs as if to stop the flow of blood, but he was immediately engulfed and toppled over by a wave of black, bristling bodies.

Another dishevelled figure buried his head in his hands and rolled himself into a ball, his frail body rocked with sobs and pleadings. The rats bit off his fingers and attacked the back of his neck as well as his exposed behind. He stayed in his foetal position as the rats ate him, still half-alive.

Myer ran. He ran faster than he'd ever run before and he almost made it. But in the dark, and in his panic, he ran into a gravestone. He somersaulted over it, landing on his back. At once, the rats were upon him, their razor-sharp teeth soon tearing his feeble old body to shreds.

Outside the ruin, on the main road, a crowd had gathered. They'd heard the screams and the commotion but none dare enter the dark churchyard. They couldn't see through the foliage, but they knew the type that made those old bomb-sites their homes and were not too anxious to investigate.

Eventually two policemen arrived, closely followed by a squad car. A powerful searchlight was directed into the under-growth, and three policemen with torches went in.

They emerged again three minutes later, all deathly pale. One went to the side of the road and vomited.

Chapter 6

Harris woke with a start and automatically reached for the shrilling alarm. The ringing always shocked him when it caught him unawares. Lately, he'd got into the habit of waking just a few minutes before the alarm went off, waiting for the first explosive ring, and shutting it off immediately with a fast-moving hand. Then he'd doze for twenty minutes or so.

But this morning, it had caught him in a deep dream. He tried to remember what it had been about. Something to do with teeth. Sharp teeth. Tearing.

Bloody hell, he thought, it was rats. Thousands of them. He'd looked out his window, he remembered, it was night-time, and there below him were thousands of rats, all perfectly still, just staring up at him in the moonlight. Thousands of wicked-looking eyes. Then they'd surged forward, crashing through the front door, scurrying up the stairs. Thank God for the alarm.

He turned over with a groan and put his arm around the curled-up figure lying next to him.

"Morning, Jude." The girl curled up into a tighter ball, murmuring softly.

Harris ran his tongue down her naked back, making her squirm with pleasure. He put his hand between her arms and drawn-up thighs and lightly stroked her smooth stomach. She languidly turned around to face him, stretching her arms and legs as she did so.

"Hello," she said as she kissed him.

He drew her close and they both stretched against each other.

"It's late," he said.

"Not that late."

"Oh yes it is." He ran his fingers along the inside of her thighs, teasing her. "Didn't you have enough last night?"

"No." She began to kiss his eyelids.

"Well, I did." He laughed as he whipped back the covers.

"Now get out in that kitchen and rattle those pots and pans."

"Pig."

He watched her as she slipped on her dressing gown and disappeared into the kitchen. As the sound of cupboards being opened and closed, water filling the kettle and Radio One music came through to him, he lay thinking of Judy.

They had lived together for six or seven months now and their love seemed to grow stronger by the day. She was a dress designer, a good one too, and they'd met at a mutual friend's party. They'd slept together that first night, but she hadn't let him make love to her. He'd tried of course, but she'd gently discouraged him, and to his amazement the next morning, he was glad she had. Weeks later, when they realised they were both in love with each other, he'd asked why she'd let him stay that first night but hadn't let him make love. She couldn't explain because she didn't really understand herself. Not the fact that they hadn't made love, but that she'd let him sleep with her. She'd never slept with anyone before, and although she'd been engaged for two years, her love-making had been confined to touching only.

It was just that she'd felt something "stir" inside her that night. She'd almost felt sorry for him in a strange way. He appeared on the surface to be self-sufficient, confident, but underneath he was the proverbial "little-boy-lost". He'd smiled

and said that was his usual trick with women but she'd nodded
and replied:

"Yes, that was quite apparent. But even underneath that,
there really was a little lost soul running around. You, Harris,
are a man of many layers."

He'd been impressed. Flattered that anyone should be interested enough to try and "suss" him out like that. She'd
gone on to explain that she couldn't let him go that night,
that she wanted to be close to him, but she couldn't let the
final barrier down until she was sure of him. And herself.

A few months later they rented a flat in the King's Cross
area and moved in together. They'd talked about marriage
and decided it wasn't important just yet. They would live together for at least a year and then decide. Either for – or
against.

Sometimes, usually when he was alone, the old hardness
would come creeping over him, and he'd say to himself: "Harris, you're onto a good thing here, son." But when he was with
Judy, walking, holding hands, making love, tenderness would
sweep away any harshness from his feelings.

Judy's voice from the kitchen interrupted his thoughts.

"Okay, lazy, breakfast's almost ready." He leapt out of
bed, shrugged on an old blue bathrobe and went into the
toilet on the landing. Then he went down to the front door to
collect the paper. When he returned, he kissed Judy's neck
and sat down at the small table.

"Good thing you called me when you did, I thought my
bladder was going to burst."

Judy placed bacon and tomatoes before him and sat down
to her hard-boiled egg. He hated eggs first thing in the morning.

He unfolded the *Mirror* to look at the headlines. He usually
read the paper on the bus on the way to school – he loved to
leave it around the staff-room, to the disapproval of his colleagues who thought any newspaper other than the *Times* or
The Guardian were comic-books – but he always glanced at
the headlines at breakfast.

"Christ, listen to this," he mumbled through a mouthful
of bread, "Six tramps eaten alive by rats. Late last night,

police were called to a bomb-site in Stepney after passers-by
had heard screams and the sounds of violent struggle coming
from the ruins of the old St. Anne's churchyard. On investigation, the police officers discovered the remains of six bodies,
apparently killed by rats, a few of which were still feeding
on the corpses. The area was immediately cordoned off, and
police, wearing protective clothing and assisted by a leading
pest extermination company, combed the ruins for the rats'
lair but were unable to discover any trace of the vermin.
Earlier in the day, Karen Blakely, aged thirteen months, and
her dog, were attacked and killed by rats in their home. The
girl's mother, Paula Blakely, is still in hospital under sedation
and is now said to be seriously ill. An inquiry committee will
be set up to. . . ."

Harris finished reading the article in silence and Judy came
round and leaned over his shoulder.

"It's awful." She shuddered and pressed close to him. "How
can that sort of thing happen in this day and age?"

"I know there's still some terrible slums left, but I didn't
realise that they were bad enough to breed anything like this."
He shook his head in puzzlement. "That must be the woman
I saw in hospital yesterday. And Keogh. He said he saw two
enormous rats. Perhaps he wasn't exaggerating after all. What
the hell's happening?"

They both got dressed and left the flat. As they were both
going in opposite directions, Harris to the East End, Judy to
the big department store for which she "created" fashions
in the West End, they kissed goodbye in the street and went
their separate ways.

On the bus Harris pondered on the question of rats and
wondered if the three incidents were connected. Was it just
coincidence or were they tied up in some way? Could it have
been the same rats or were they different groups? He decided
he'd question Keogh further about his two rats when he remembered the boy wouldn't be in that day. Well, never mind,
tomorrow would do.

But there wasn't a tomorrow for Keogh. When Harris
reached the school he was called into the principal's office and
told that the boy had been rushed to hospital the previous

night with a severe fever and was at that moment in a critical condition. The hospital had rung and asked if anyone else had been with him when he'd been bitten by the rat? And could the teacher who had brought him to the hospital yesterday come along to see them?

"Yes, I'll just get my class organized and I'll go over right away," Harris said to the worried-looking Mr. Norton.

"No, I've seen to that," said the headmaster. "You get going now. They insisted it was urgent. Try not to be too long."

Harris left the school and made towards the hospital at a brisk pace. When he arrived he began to explain who he was but the receptionist had been expecting him and immediately took him to an office near the rear of the building where he was asked to wait. He had barely sat down when the door opened and three men strode in.

"Ah, you're the boy's teacher?" enquired the first man, walking around to the desk. His portly figure lowered itself into a chair with a weary slump and his tired eyes barely flickered towards Harris. He waved his hand at the two others before Harris could reply. "Doctor Strackley" – the doctor nodded – "and Mr. Foskins from the Ministry of Health." Foskins stretched a hand towards the teacher who shook it. "And my name is Tunstall, I'm the Hospital Group Secretary." The man behind the desk finished his introductions glancing through a sheaf of papers. He stopped at one in particular, seemingly studying it closely, but at the same time asking, "Your name?"

"Harris. How is Keogh?"

Tunstall looked up from his document. "You haven't been told?"

Harris froze at the tone of the group secretary's voice.

"I'm afraid he died during the night."

Harris shook his head in disbelief. "But it was only yesterday that he was bitten."

"Yes, we know, Mr. Harris," the doctor stepped forward and leaned on the desk, his eyes looking intently at the stunned teacher. "That's why we asked you to come along. You brought the boy here yesterday. Perhaps you could tell us how and where he received the bite?"

"But you can't die just from a bite. And in one day?" Harris shook his head at the three men, ignoring the doctor's question.

Tunstall spoke up, putting the papers finally to one side. "No, it seems impossible, doesn't it? A post mortem is already being carried out to see if Keogh was suffering from any other illness at the time. We thought possibly the bite may have acted as some kind of catalyst for a hidden disease carried by the boy. But we've virtually discounted that theory now, although we're still checking it out. You see, a woman was brought in yesterday too – you may have read about it in the papers; her child was killed by rats – and she was herself attacked by them in an attempt to save her daughter. She died two hours ago."

"But that means anyone who comes in contact with the rats and gets bitten by one ..." before Harris could finish, Foskins interrupted.

"Yes, Mr. Harris. Once a person has been bitten, they have about twenty-four hours to live. That's why it's essential to learn as much as possible about these particular rats. They're obviously an unknown species, unknown to us in England anyway. From what we've heard, their sheer size is quite extraordinary ..."

"We want to know everything the boy told you of the incident," said Tunstall impatiently.

"Yes, of course," Harris nodded. "But how did they die? What did they die of?" He looked at each of the three men in turn. The room filled with an uneasy silence.

Finally, the doctor cleared his throat and looked at the group secretary. "I think it's only fair that we take Mr. Harris into our confidence. I think we can trust him to be discreet, and he may be able to help us if he knows this area well."

"I was born here. I know most of this region – and I know exactly where Keogh saw his rats."

"Very well," sighed Tunstall. "But understand, you must not repeat anything said in this room to anybody. We're not sure what we're up against yet, and until we are, we must treat it with the utmost discretion. We don't want people to panic over something that may only be a rare occurrence."

"Like six tramps being eaten alive," interjected Harris.

"Yes, yes, Mr. Harris, we know it's a bit frightening," said Foskins quickly. "But we don't want people panicking do we? I mean, the first thing to suffer would be the docks, wouldn't it? Heaven knows, the dockers don't need much excuse to stay away from work so just think of what this sort of scare could do. And if foodstuff were left to rot in the warehouses and ships, what then? The whole waterfront would be infested within a few days. Vicious circle, Mr. Harris, vicious circle."

The teacher remained silent.

"Look, we'll probably overcome this problem before anything else occurs," Tunstall leaned forward, pointing a finger at Harris. "Now your help isn't essential, but if you do want to assist us you must agree to silence."

What brought that on wondered Harris. He must be really worried. "All right," he shrugged. "I just want to know how Keogh and the woman died."

"Of course," smiled Doctor Strackley, trying to break the icy atmosphere. "The deaths were caused by an infection introduced by the bite of the rat into the bloodstream. The usual disease caused by the vermin is called Weil's Disease, Leptrospirosis or Spirochoetal Jaundice. We only have about ten or eleven cases of this a year in this country – it's that rare. The organism that causes it, Leptospira Ictero-haemorrhagae, is carried by rats and conveyed to man in their urine, either through the skin or alimentary tract. It's an occupational hazard to workers in sewers. Incubation period is from seven to thirteen days; onset of the disease is abrupt fever, muscular pains, loss of appetite and vomiting. The feverish stage lasts several days before jaundice appears and the patient becomes prostrate. Temperature usually declines in about ten days but relapses tend to occur. We often treat the disease by penicillin and other antibiotics but we do have a special serum for it. Trouble is, it's rarely diagnosed as Weil's Disease in time to use it.

"Right, so that's the disease we know about. Now, the incredible thing about last night's two cases is that the whole process happened within twenty-four hours." He paused, as if for effect. "There are other differences too."

He looked at Tunstall, silently seeking permission to carry on. Tunstall nodded.

"The fever strikes within five or six hours. Jaundice sets in immediately. The victim rapidly loses all his senses – sight goes first. The body goes into a coma, occasionally being racked by violent spasms. Then, the most horrible thing happens. The skin – by now completely yellow – becomes taut. It becomes thinner as it stretches over the bone structure. It turns to a fine tissue. Finally, it begins to tear. Gaping holes appear all over the body. The poor victim dies a terribly painful death, which even our strongest drugs seem only to ease a little."

The three men remained silent as the knowledge sought entry into Harris's numbed brain.

"Poor Keogh," he finally said.

"Yes, and God help anybody else who gets bitten," said Tunstall, almost impatiently. "Now, before anything else happens, we're getting the Ratkill people in. They're a good company and very discreet. They're investigating the bomb-site and the woman's home this morning and if you can tell us where the boy was bitten, we'll get them to have a look around that area too."

Harris told them about the old canal that Keogh had been using as a short cut. "Look, let me take some of the exterminators down there, I can show them the exact spot."

"Yes," said Foskins, "we're going along to the church-yard now to see how they're getting on. You can come along and then take some of their chaps off to the canal."

"I'll have to ring the school first."

"All right, but not a word to anyone about this. Just say the hospital needs you for a statement. Now when you do go back to your school we'd like you to ask your pupils if they've seen any rats recently, and if so, where. Also, if they're bitten by anything – anything at all – they're to go straight to the hospital. If you can tell this without frightening them, we'd appreciate it."

"It would take more than that to frighten my bunch," smiled Harris.

"I think it was around here," Harris told the one Ratkill man

he'd been allowed to take away from the chaotic and gruesome churchyard scene. He and the rodent exterminator, a
quiet little man whose thin, pointed face, Harris mused, was
not far off resembling the creature he was paid to obliterate,
were now standing before a high brick wall.

"The canal's on the other side," said Harris. "If we walk
down a bit, we'll come to railings, and unless it has changed
now, there'll be a few openings."

As they walked the little man, whose name was Albert Ferris, lost some of his reserve and slight wariness of Harris's
profession and began to talk to the teacher.

"I've never seen anything like that place this morning, you
know. I've been at this game for fifteen years and never seen
anything like it. Blood, and bits of bodies, all over the place.
Terrible. But no rats. None dead, you know. Those poor old
buggers couldn't have known what hit them. Mind you, they
were probably all well gone on that stuff they drink, all well
boozed. But all the same, you'd have thought at least one of
them would have got out of it. Or killed some of the rats anyway." He shook his head. "Beats me.'

"I've never heard of rats actually attacking people for food
before," said Harris, to keep the man talking. He was determined to learn as much as possible about the situation. He
didn't know why, but the uneasiness he felt went deeper than
the natural abhorrence of the shocking tragedy.

"No, they don't as a rule," Ferris replied. "Not in this
country anyway. You see rats are very, very cautious. They
can live on practically anything and they certainly wouldn't
attack just for flesh, you know. Corpses, yes. They'd eat corpses. But attack a man just for food? No. But, what puzzled us
this morning was some of the spoors we found. Twice as large
as normal rats' droppings. We've sent them off to the lab to
have them analyzed, but what they obviously suggest is very
large rats. And now, if London's started breeding a colony of
bigger-than-average rats – and you know how fast they breed
– well, I reckon we're in for a lot of bother. And if they're
attacking people . . ." He shook his head again.

"Just how fast do they breed, in fact?" asked the teacher.

"The female can have from five to eight litters a year, with

anything from four to twelve in a litter. Then the randy buggers are at it again after a couple of hours. I don't much fancy
mobs of them big ones roaming around."

Nor did Harris.

They came to the railings and found an opening.

"Look," Harris said to Ferris, "you know we're only looking for signs of these creatures – we don't actually want to
catch any."

"Don't worry, mate, I'm not going to tangle with them."

Assured he was on no crusade mission with the little man,
Harris led the way through the gap. They slowly began to
walk back towards the starting point of the wall, keeping a
wary eye for any small movement.

Ferris was the first to see them. He'd been scrutinising the
far bank, looking for any dark holes, groups of droppings,
anything at all, when his gaze fell upon three moving objects
in the dark waters. Against the dark brown muddy canal
water could be seen three small, black heads gliding in the
opposite direction to which they were walking.

"Look," he pointed excitedly. "Three of them"

Harris looked across to where Ferris was pointing. He saw
the three black shapes instantly, their perfect triangular formation causing smooth water-trails behind them.

"All right, let's follow them."

"They seem to know where they're going!" Harris called
back to the little rat-killer, who was having a hard time keeping up with him.

Suddenly, the dark creatures emerged from the water and
scurried up the bank. For the first time, the two men could see
the whole of their bodies.

"Christ, they're enormous" exclaimed Harris.

"I've never seen any that size before," Ferris said, open-
mouthed. "We'd better keep clear of them for the moment,
mate. We don't want to, er, excite them."

"We'll have to try to follow them," said Harris firmly.
"They may lead us to their lair."

As he spoke, the leading rat stopped and turned his head
towards them. The other two froze and did the same.

Harris would never forget the horror he felt under the gaze

of the three pairs of sharp, wicked-looking eyes. It wasn't just their size, or natural repulsion of vermin that numbed him. It was because they didn't run, or try to hide. There was no sign of panic. Just three still bodies, malevolently watching the two men, as though deciding whether to swim across to them or go on their way. Harris knew if there were any hint of the foul creatures making towards them, he would not hesitate to run as fast as his legs would carry him. He guessed when Ferris' hand gripped his arm that the rat-killer had the same idea.

But the rats suddenly turned and disappeared through a hole in the old wooden fence that protected that side of the canal from public property.

"Thank Gawd for that." Ferris exhaled a deep mouthful of air. And then, when he'd recovered slightly; "what's over there?"

Harris thought for a moment, trying to recollect the surrounding area. "Well, there's a bit of wasteland – we can see the undergrowth from here – and then there's. . . ." He scratched his cheek and pondered. "Oh, no. Flats. There's blocks of flats behind the waste. Fortunately most of the kids will be at school although some may be coming home for dinner around this time. My guess is that the rats are making for the big rubbish bins that belong to the flats. We'll have to get around there fast, just in case."

As he was about to run along the iron fence on their side of the canal to find an opening, his eyes caught more movement in the water. This time coming from the opposite direction of the first three, he saw a bigger group of black shapes gliding through the water. He registered at least seven before he began running after Ferris, whose reaction to the fearsome pack was immediate.

As he ran, Harris glanced back to see the furry, wet bodies scurrying through the same hole in the fence that the other three had used.

When the two shaken men reached the road once again, Harris pulled the little exterminator to a halt.

"Look, get onto the police," he said, his lungs gasping for air. "Get them to contact your people and get them over here as fast as possible. I'm going around to the flats, you follow when you've 'phoned. There's a small road bridge across the canal not far in that direction, so follow me as fast as possible, for Christ's sake. I don't want to come up against that lot on my own!"

"Look, mate, rats are my business," Ferris answered back fiercely."You go get the police. I'll find out where they're going to and I'll know how to handle them when I do. I'm no hero, but it's bloody commonsense ain't it?"

Without waiting for a reply, the little man set off at a jogging pace.

Who's arguing? thought Harris to himself and began to look around for a 'phone box.

The rats sped swiftly through the undergrowth, joined now by groups of the smaller variety. They reached another wooden fence that separated the council tenements from the wasteland. They flowed under through its many gaps and made towards the large waste-disposal bunkers that stood at the bottom of each block of flats. Food and litter of all kinds were emptied down the chutes from all floors of the block by its residents into a huge round bin that was cleared by the council's sanitation department each week. Many a family pet was buried in this way when their lives ended either by accident or from old age. Potato peelings, egg-shells, stale food, paper, anything that could fit into the chute was disposed of in this way, and allowed to mix and rot for a week before being emptied into and then churned up by the grinding dust-cart. By the end of the week the smell was always abominable and residents warned their young to stay away from the rotting doors of the bunkers.

It was the first time a large group of rats had visited the site during the day. Usually there were too many children laughing, screaming, fighting, making noise because of the sheer delight of making noise, for the people-shy beasts. The night was their ally.

But now they had a new boldness. Led by the bigger, blacker rats, a species that had suddenly appeared amongst them, to dominate and intimidate, they had found a new courage. Or at least, a new driving force.

So far unseen they sped along the walls of the buildings in single file until they reached a bunker where many nights before, they had gnawed holes in the doors to provide access for their ever-hungry bodies. They hurriedly passed through and then into the holes, again made by themselves, beneath the vast cylinder of rubbish, and so into the heap itself, gnawing, eating anything that could be chewed.

The big rats were the first to know it was there. Somebody had deposited their weekend joint into the chute. Perhaps it had been rotten, perhaps a husband, tired of being chastised for not being home from the pub on time for his Sunday lunch had thrown the whole joint away in a fit of rage. But there it was, and the rats lust for meat was aroused to a frightening degree.

The smaller rats tried to get at the meat but were instantly killed and then devoured by their superiors.

Ferris heard the squeals of the lesser rats as he ran past the bunker. He stopped dead and listened intently, his sharp little face turned to one side. Then he realized where the noise was coming from. Slowly, and very quietly he walked towards the seemingly solid doors. The smell of stale food assured him of the worst. He spotted the holes at the bottom of the doors and carefully got down on one knee. He listened again. Silence, now. He cautiously lowered his head towards the larger of the black holes and tried to peer into the darkness. Nothing moved. He was down on both knees now, his right ear almost touching the ground.

The huge rat flew out at him without warning and bit deep into the flesh of his cheek. Ferris screamed and fell back, beating wildly at the creature on his face. With all his strength he pulled the rat away from him, tearing a gaping hole in his cheek, but he couldn't hold the powerful, wriggling body and it fell upon him once more. The other rodents came streaming through the holes at the little man, whose screaming had started to bring people to their doors and windows.

When the residents saw the white overalled figure on the floor, surrounded and covered with dark, furry bodies, they could not quite believe what was happening. Some, once they realized, slammed their doors, and for some reason bolted them, as though they thought the strange creatures could pick locks. Others – they were mostly women, their husbands being at work – screamed or fainted. Some who had 'phones, rang for the police. Many just stared in horror-struck silence. One old pensioner, a stout but active woman, ran forward brandishing a broom above her head. She brought it down heavily on the nearest bodies to her, these being the smaller rats on the outer fringes of the circle around the struggling man. As they scattered, a larger rat stopped its gorging and turned a menacing eye towards her.

The first phone box Harris found had been wrecked by vandals. Knowing other boxes in the area would probably have been tampered with, he decided to waste no more time but to try the nearest shop or pub. He found a tobacconists and hastily asked the proprietor permission to 'phone for the police. The shopkeeper was a trifle wary at first but the teacher's earnestness convinced him that the young man was on the level.

When the call was made and directions given, Harris thanked the tobacconist and left the shop at a run. He soon reached the spot where he and Ferris had split up and headed in the direction that the little rat-exterminator had gone. He crossed the canal bridge and saw the council flats before him. He heard the commotion seconds before he came upon the ghastly scene. As he ran into the grounds and turned a corner he saw an old lady, furiously waving a broom in the air, being dragged to the ground by several large rats. Harris was frozen to the spot until her pitiful cries for help spurred him forward, only too aware of the lethal disease the rat-bites carried, but knowing he couldn't just stand by and watch the old lady be torn to pieces. Fortunately for Harris, a group of workmen from a nearby building-site had heard the screams, and were now advancing on the rats armed with picks, shovels, anything that had come to hand in their rush to the buildings.

Again the large rat that had observed the old pensioner now looked up and furtively studied the approaching men. The other, bigger rats, also stopped their frenzied attack.

This did not deter the workmen. They advanced, shouting and waving their assorted weapons.

Suddenly, as though in one body, the rats turned and fled, leaving their smaller companions to the merciless onslaught of the enraged men.

Harris backed up against the wall as he saw the creatures fleeing in his direction. They scurried past him, one actually running over his shoe, causing him to shudder involuntarily. Another stopped before him, eyed him coolly for a fraction of a second, and then sped on its way. Harris almost collapsed with relief as the last horrifying shape disappeared beneath the fence of the wasteground. It looked as though two of the workmen were about to climb the fence to follow them, but Harris managed to find his voice in time to stop them.

As they walked back the teacher was able to turn his gaze back towards the carnage the rats had caused. The old lady was on the ground, her chest heaving in sharp, uneven movements, covered in blood, still feebly holding onto the broom. It was only then that Harris saw the shredded, blood-stained overalls of little Ferris. It was only the now barely recognizable uniform with its "Ratkill" logo emblazoned on the chest that made him realize it was the little rat exterminator, for the crumpled body no longer had a face.

"Get an ambulance, quickly," Harris said weakly to one of the workmen, knowing already it was too late for the old woman.

"There's one on the way," one of her neighbours came forward. The others now began to slowly emerge from their homes and tentatively walked towards the bodies, keeping a wary eye on the fence.

"What were they?" someone asked.

"Rats, weren't they," another replied.

"What – that size?" the first person again.

"Big as dogs."

"Come on, let's go after them," the workman who had been prepared to climb the fence growled. "We can't have things like them running around."

"No," said Harris. He couldn't tell them about the fatal disease the vermin carried, but he had to stop them from trying to do battle with them. "The police are on their way, and the people from Ratkill too, better let them deal with them."

"Time we wait for the law, the bleeders'll have disappeared. I'm going now. Who else is coming?"

Harris caught him by the arm as he began to march towards the fence. As he angrily swung around, two police cars roared into the estate and came to a screeching halt beside the group of stricken people.

Foskins emerged from the second car and strode directly towards Harris, his eyes never leaving the two figures on the ground.

As a Ratkill van arrived, he pulled the teacher to one side so the gathering crowd would be unable to hear their conversation.

"Well, Mr. Harris, what happened?"

The teacher briefly told him of the events just past. He felt full of pity for the little rat-faced Ferris whose sense of duty towards his job had led to his untimely death. It could have been Harris, himself, lying there if Ferris hadn't insisted on following the rats himself.

"We'll get a search party down there immediately," Foskins told him. "They'll go through the fence and down the canal. We'll send out patrols along the canal and cordon the area off."

"Look, these canals run for miles. How can you possibly cordon them off?" Harris was slightly irritated by Foskins' calm, authoritatively calm, voice. "And in any case, how are you going to cordon off all the sewers that run beneath this area?"

"That, Mr. Harris," said Foskins coldly, "is *our* problem."

Chapter 7

Harris was in no mood to go back to the school that afternoon. He walked for a while through the streets of his childhood, coming upon long-forgotten alleys; a tobacconist where he bought his first packet of "Domino" cigarettes; Linda Crossley's house, a girl who had one night, when they were teenagers, let he and six of his mates have it off with her at the back of their local youth club – and was forever after known as "7-up"; bomb-sites, still untouched by building developments; stunted posts, once used to tie horses to, in his day to play leap-frog and today – well, not many horses around any more – and when was the last time he'd seen kids playing leap-frog? Finally, he caught a bus and returned to the flat. He made himself some tea and sat in his only armchair, still depressed by the morning's events. Keogh, the woman and her baby, those poor old down-and-outs, Ferris and the old lady. Civilised London. Swinging London. Dirty bloody London!

For all its modernity, its high standard of living, it could still breed obnoxious, disease-carrying vermin of the like he'd seen today. And their size! What had caused this mutation?

And their cunning. Twice that day, one of the big, black rats had just stood and stared at him (had it been the same one each time? Christ!) not cowering, nor preparing to attack, but just surveying him, seemingly studying him, inscrutable.

How many more people would they kill before they were put down? And where had they come from? What made them so much more intelligent than their smaller counterparts? Well, why should he worry. It was the problem of the bloody authorities. But what disgusted him more? The vermin themselves – or the fact that it could only happen in East London? Not Hampstead or Kensington, but Poplar. Was it the old prejudices against the middle and upper classes, the councils that took the working-class from their slums and put them into tall, remote concrete towers, telling them they'd never been better off, but never realizing that forty homes in a block of flats became forty separate cells for people, communication between them confined to conversations in the lift, was it this that really angered him? That these same councils could allow the filth that could produce vermin such as the black rats. He remembered the anger he'd felt at the time a new "ultra-modern" flat had collapsed when by some miracle only nine people had been killed. His resentment had been directed not only at the architects who had designed the "block" construction, but at the council who had approved its design. He remembered the rumours that had spread afterwards, the favourite being the one about the safe-breaker who had kept gelignite in his flat, and it had been this that had exploded and forced out one of the concrete slabs, causing the walls down one side to topple like a pack of cards. Then it had been the gas leak, which had, in fact, been proved as the cause. But the point was it was the construction itself that had made a minor disaster into a major one. And the construction had been a cheaper means of building – a cheaper way of cramming thirty or forty families into the smallest square footage possible. This is what embittered Harris. The incompetence of "authority."

Then he had to smile at himself. He was still a student at heart, a rebel against the powers that be. As a teacher, he was directly under the control of a government body and was

often exasperated by "committee" decisions, but he knew
there were fair-minded men and women who really did care
amongst the committee members, who fought hard to get the
right decisions. He'd heard many stories of individuals who
had fought the government ban on free milk for kids, for instance. Of men and women, including teachers, who had all-
but lost their jobs because of their opposition.

No, it was no good becoming over-wrought with authority,
for he knew too well that apathy existed on all levels. The gas-
man who neglected to fix a leaky pipe. The mechanic who
failed to tighten a screw. The driver who drove at fifty miles
an hour in the fog. The milkman who left one pint instead of
two. It was a matter of degree. Wasn't that what Original Sin
was supposed to be all about? We're all to blame. He fell
asleep.

At a quarter-past-six, he was awakened by the front door
being slammed and footsteps racing up the stairs.

"Hello, Jude," he said as she bustled in, red-faced and
breathless.

"Hello, lazy," she kissed his nose. "Have you seen the paper
yet?" She unfolded a Standard and showed him the headlines
proclaiming more killings by rats.

"Yes, I know. I was there." He told her of the day's events,
his voice hard, emotionless.

"Oh, love, it's horrible. Those poor people. And you. It
must have been terrible for you." She touched his cheek,
knowing his anger covered up deeper feelings.

"I'm just sick of it, Jude. For people to die senselessly like
that in this day and age. It's crazy."

"All right, darling. They'll soon put a stop to it. It's not like
the old days, when things like this got out of hand."

"That's not the point though. It should never have happened in the first place."

Suddenly Harris relaxed, his natural defence when events
became too much to take. He reached a certain point, and
knowing there was nothing he could do about the situation,
his mind walked away from it.

He smiled at Judy. "Let's get away from it at the weekend.

eh? Let's go and see your silly old aunt at Walton. The fresh
air will do us both good."

"Okay," Judy's arms encircled his neck and she squeezed it
hard.

"What's for dinner?" he asked.

The rest of the week, as far as the rats were concerned, was
quiet. There had been a public outcry, the usual campaigns
from the press to clean up London. Angry debates on television by politicians and councillors, and even a statement
from the Prime Minister. Large areas of dockland were sealed
off and rat-exterminators sent in. The dockers themselves
came out on strike for two days until they had been convinced
that no trace of rats could be found. Canals leading to the
docks were searched by police and soldiers, but nothing larger
than the usual rodents were found, and not many of these
either. Reports of large, black rats being seen came in regularly, but on investigation it usually turned out to be a dog or
cat. Children were escorted to and from schools by parents
if any quiet street were on the journey. Bomb-sites and playgrounds became unusually still. Pet shops all over London
did a booming trade in cats and dogs. Poisons were laid by
the experts, but the victims were always mice or the usual
smaller rat.

Not one large, black rat was found.

People soon began to lose interest, as other news hit the
headlines. Stories of rape, robbery, and arson, political and
non-political, took over as conversation points. Although the
search still went on, chemicals laid to poison the rats, and still
nothing was found, no deaths occurred, the matter was considered to have been dealt with. Foskins was still uneasy, and
made sure his department was following the matter right
through to the end; the end being the extinction of any vermin likely to cause damage to persons or property. It soon
became apparent, however, that it would be a virtually impossible task unless more government aid was given, but as
the outcry dwindled, so did talk of money from the ex-
chequer's purse.

Chapter 8

On Friday evening, Harris and Judy drove down to Walton in their battered old Hillman Minx. Judy's aunt made a great fuss of them when they arrived and proved herself to be not as silly as Harris believed by showing them into a quaint, but comfortable room with a double bed. She left them as they unpacked their one case all three of them smiling inanely at each other.

"Well, well, good old Aunt Hazel," grinned Harris as Judy flopped onto the ancient quilt, whooping with glee.

"She always was my favourite aunt," she giggled, as Harris stretched beside her.

She smacked his exploring hands. "Come on, let's unpack and go down before she regrets giving us a room together because of lack of company."

When they went downstairs, Judy's aunt had opened a bottle of sherry. She poured them a drink and bade them sit down on a soft, flower-patterned sofa, seating herself in an armchair opposite them. As she chattered on, questioning them about their jobs, gossiping about her neighbours, reliving the times she'd had with Judy's mother, Harris felt himself relaxing.

His arm found its way around Judy's shoulders, her fingers found his. He laughed at the silliest topics of Aunt Hazel, losing himself in the charm and the enclosed world of village life. He found himself deeply interested in the vicar's jumble sale tomorrow morning; the widow next door's fancy-man; the donkey-derby held last week. He found himself laughing not at the old aunt, but with her, envying the uncomplicated life she led.

At half-past ten, she suggested that the young couple should go for a brief stroll before going to bed, the exercise would make them sleep better. They walked arm in arm through the quiet village, both sensing the feeling of peace within each other.

"Deep breaths," said Harris, taking in a huge lungful of air.

They both took several more exaggerated deep breaths, faces raised towards the million visible stars, finally bursting into laughter at their own earnest efforts. They walked on, the stillness around them mellowing their already soft mood.

"Maybe I could get a position in a school outside London," mused Harris. "In a village like this. Or maybe even open a post office. What do you think"

Judy smiled back at him, knowing how he loved to dream like this. He was a city person basically, although often he told her how he disliked it. "All right, and I'll open a little dress shop, you know, all tweeds and woollies. But I don't know what the vicar would say about us living together. He'd probably think I was a scarlet woman."

"Well, we could humour him and get married."

They stopped walking and Judy turned round to face him, "You make any more offers like that, Harris, and I'll make you stick to them."

When they returned to Aunt Hazel's, they found hot toast and drinking chocolate waiting for them. The old aunt fluttered around in a long dressing gown, still chattering on about anything that came into her head, then bade them goodnight and disappeared up the stairs.

"She's lovely," grinned Harris, sipping his hot chocolate. "She'd drive me mad, but she's lovely."

When they finally went upstairs, they discovered a hot-water bottle tucked into the bed and a fire alight in the hearth. Harris couldn't stop smiling as they undressed. It was a long time since either of them had been spoilt and it was nice now that they were being spoilt together.

He climbed in beside Judy and drew her warm body towards him. "I wish we could stay longer. I'm going to hate going back."

"Let's enjoy what we've got, darling. We've got the whole weekend." Judy's sensitive fingers glided down his back causing him to shiver. They crept, round to his thigh and then up.

"Judy, Judy, Judy," Cary Grant voice. "What would the vicar say?"

The next day they were awakened by a careful tap on the door. Aunt Hazel entered with a tray of tea and biscuits and the morning paper for Harris. They thanked her trying to keep themselves covered up as she bustled about the room, drawing the curtains, retrieving the cast-out hot-water bottle. As she rambled on with her inexhaustible comments on the weather, the neighbours and the state of Mrs Green's cabbage patch, Judy began pinching Harris' naked bottom beneath the blankets. Trying hard not to yelp, he grabbed her wrist and sat on her hand. Then he began plucking at the small mound of hair between her thighs.

When Judy could no longer refrain from crying out loud, she had to explain to her surprised aunt, between fits of laughter, that she had cramp in her foot. Aunt Hazel's hand shot beneath the bed clothes, grabbed Judy's foot and began rubbing vigorously. By this time, Harris was choking with glee and had to hide behind his trembling newspaper.

At ten, they dressed and went down to breakfast. The aunt asked them what they were going to do with themselves all day, suggesting they might like to come along to the jumble-sale. They excused themselves by saying they wanted to drive into Stratford to have a look around, and would probably stay there for lunch. After warning them to be careful of the roads, she perched a jaunty straw hat on her head, grabbed her shopping basket and waved her goodbyes, turning at the garden gate to wave at them again. They washed the dishes and while Judy remade their bed, Harris cleared the grate downstairs and a new fire was laid. Although he couldn't imagine why the old girl would want a fire in this weather, he had to admit it made a welcoming sight in the evening.

Eventually, they climbed into their car and drove towards Stratford, singing at the top of their voices as they made their way along the country lanes.

As soon as Harris had trouble in finding a parking space he began to regret their visit to the old town of Stratford. It was flooded with people, cars and coaches. He'd never been there before and had expected to find quaint, olde-worlde, oak-beamed houses in cobbled streets. Angry with himself for his naïvete, for not realising a tourist-attraction centre like this must surely be spoiled by commercialism he finally found a back street to park in. Walking towards the Royal Shakespeare Theatre he saw that many of the streets had managed to retain their old charm, after all, but it was the throngs of people, multi-racial accents, that destroyed any hope of atmosphere. And the nearer the theatre they got, so the noisier the streets became.

A thin, sallow-looking round-shouldered man in an open-necked, short-sleeved, floppy shirt, camera hanging on his flat chest: "Are you coomin',: Ilda?"

The droning reply, from a plump, bespectacled woman emerging from a shop doorway, clutching a dozen Stratford-on-Avon postcards. "Wait, oop, wait oop."

An obvious Yank, short-cropped hair, checked jacket, inevitable camera: "Will ya look at that, Immogene. Quick, while I take a shot."

Immogene posing self-consciously before an oaked-beamed shop with a thatched roof, licking an ice cream, magnified eyes peering through blue-tinted butterfly glasses: "Wilya' hurry up, Mervyn, I feel stupid."

They arrived at the Theatre, a heavy depressing building, and found it closed.

"Let's take a boat down the river," Judy suggested tentatively sensing Harris' disappointment. But the river itself was swarming with punts, canoes and row-boats.

"Let's have a drink." Harris turned towards the nearest
pub, passing windows full of people devouring Wimpies and
sausage, egg and chips. They entered a dark bar, all wood
and stone floors. The barmaids were wearing period costumes
and smiling cheerfully as they coped with the crowds. This is
more like it, he thought, ordering a pint of Brown, a red wine
and two ham and tomato sandwiches, and took the wine over
to Judy who was sitting on a bench seat at an old round oak
table and returned for the beer. Sitting next to her, he
squeezed her hand to show her his mood was no reflection on
her.

"This isn't so bad, is it?" He turned to study a large square
timber coming from the floor and supporting the low ceiling. He reached out to let his fingers run along the deep grain.

Plastic. "Shit!"

As they left the pub, it began to drizzle with rain. Although
it was a fairly light shower, shop doorways became crowded
with people. Plastic macks appeared and were draped over
heads and shoulders. Harris and Judy were bumped by tour-
ists running for cover.

"Let's go, Jude," said Harris, taking her arm firmly and
leading her into the road. They quickly walked back to the
car, both fighting the feeling of claustrophobia. They sat in
the car and caught their breath. Harris was half-way through
a cigarette when the sun came out and the rain stopped.
People emerged from their shelters, laughing and calling to
one another. A coach pulled up on the opposite side of the
road and unloaded a stream of sight-seers, all stretching, and
yawning, and looking for the toilets.

"Look at those women," the teacher said in amazement.
"They all look the same. They're all fat, and they're all wearing glasses. I don't believe it!"

Judy burst into laughter. He was right. They *did* all look
alike. For some reason, he felt better. At least he saw the joke
of his shattered illusion of Shakespeare's birth-place. He drove
out of the crowded town, heading into the country.

As they left the town behind he felt a deep sense of relief.
He could breathe again. He didn't fully understand why the

crowds had affected him so much. He'd had a feeling of revulsion towards the people, not as individuals, but en masse. Strangely enough, it had been slightly akin to the revulsion he'd felt towards the rats. As though they were a threat.

"Jude, I'm not becoming a head-case am I?"

"No, darling. You just came into contact with too many people at the wrong time and in the wrong place. The point of coming here was to get away from it all and we ran slam-bang right into the middle of it again."

The quieter the roads became, the freer he felt. Ahead they spotted a high-curving hill, the top crowned with trees and cultivated fields below, its shades ranging from the brightest yellow to the deepest green. Sheep grazed on the wilder middle slopes.

"Fancy a climb?" Harris asked Judy.

"Okay."

He pulled over onto a grassy verge and locked the car. They climbed a fence and skirted around the edges of the field, Judy explaining the difference between wheat, corn and barley, Harris enjoying his ignorance.

Watched by the sheep they climbed over a gate, the hill now becoming much steeper. As they got nearer the top, the exertion began to tell and they laughingly clung to each other, occasionally pulling the other down. Finally they reached the trees and found a path leading through them to the summit. Here was a plateau of still more fields, stretching across to the downward slopes and shading into woods again.

Lying back on the grassy slope, they rested, taking in the surrounding hills, the tiny houses, the grey lines that were roads. A slight breeze stirred the otherwise warm air.

"Better now?" Judy asked.

"Yes."

"Deep breaths."

He reached for her. "It's so quiet. No people. It somehow puts everything into its right perspective."

A sheep, lost from its flock scampered past them. Once past, it turned and bleated at them, then ran off.

"And you," shouted Harris.

He turned to Judy and kissed her, first softly, small tender kisses, just touching her lips – then hard, urgent. His hand crept to her small, round breast beneath the jumper.

"Harris, someone might come," she warned.

"Up here," he scoffed. "You're joking. Who'd be silly enough to climb all the way up here?"

He pulled at the zipper of her trousers. She kissed his face, his neck, her love for him stirring her desire, pushing her body towards him in rhythmic motion. He tugged at the trousers, her body lifting to help him, then ran his fingers lightly over her smooth thighs. He bowed down to kiss them, his tongue creating thin moist trails along each limb. His hand began to stroke the fine material of her panties – then between her thighs.

She moaned with pleasure and reached for him, loosening his clothes, setting him free. His hand crept slowly between her flimsy panties and soft skin, finding her private silky hair, then down, between her thighs, his fingers becoming wet from her. He pulled the panties gently down her long legs and lay them to one side with her now discarded trousers. He half-sat, gazing down at her, taking pleasure from the sight of her naked thighs against the rich green grass.

She pulled him down to her. "Darling," she whispered, not really caring, "someone might see us."

"Not up here. Nobody can see us up here."

He moved into her, very gently, and very slowly. Then they clung to each other, her legs slightly bent, feet flat against the slope. He began to move back and forth inside her, their passion, as so often, equally matched. She thrust up at him, both now losing themselves in the sweetness of physical love.

But as their motions became more frantic, so his toes and knees began to loose their grip on the grassy slope. He began to slip down. He wriggled forward again grabbing tufts of grass to pull himself up. But as soon as they resumed he began to slip down again, this time losing her. He wasn't amused as she was.

"We'll have to turn around," he said, struggling back inside her. They carefully inched their way round, anti-clockwise, desperately trying to keep together, now both laughing at the ridiculous spectacle they must have made. "I can feel the blood rushing to my head," she giggled.

"I won't tell you where it's rushing to in me" he groaned, trying hard not to topple forward over her body. He held onto the grass, pushing against it now, the strain on his arms becoming more intense as their bodies sped towards their crescendoes. She writhed under him, a couple of times nearly sending him over her and rolling down the hill. They reached their climax, Harris almost with relief, and, still together, let themselves slide languidly down a few feet, bodies turning.

They rested for a few minutes, their bodies relishing the warm sun, enjoying the light breeze on their nakedness.

"I love you, darling," Judy said.

"Good, because I love you."

Reluctantly, they dressed, and Harris lit a cigarette. Judy settled back against him and they both studied the cobalt sky.

A voice broke through their tranquil thoughts.

"Susan, don't go too far, poppet!"

They both sat up and turned their heads towards the sound. A young girl of about seven came skipping over the brow of the hill, closely followed by a man and a woman who wondered why the young couple sitting on the hillside had burst into laughter.

Chapter 9

Dave Moodie lounged against the wall of the dingy Underground platform, occasionally tilting his head back and drinking from a carton of milk. I'm pissed off with this lark, he told himself, peering into the gloom of the colourless station. Seeing the same girl, three times a week, for two months now, was a bit strong. Pictures Wednesday, club Saturday, telly Sunday; and now she wanted him to cut out his Friday night football. Some chance! It wasn't as though they were even engaged, but Gerry was becoming more and more possessive, laying down the law about his friends, finding fault in his clothes, picking him up on his language. And all this performance; running to catch his last train, racing down those treacherous steps of Shadwell tube, a couple of times missing one and nearly breaking an ankle. He wouldn't mind but he'd spent the whole evening groping and trying to get her worked up but getting nowhere, and then, when it was time to go, she'd suddenly turn on and start getting fruity. His mates had told him she was a P.T., prick-teaser, but he hadn't believed them, in fact, he'd even belted one of them.

"Maybe I'll give her the shove next week," he said to himself, voicing his thoughts for extra assurance. He began to whistle. But it was funny how he looked forward to seeing her by the time Wednesday came round. He stopped whistling. She always looked good, always dressed smart. Her mother got on his nerves, but he rarely saw her. Her father was a lazy old bastard too. Not like his mum and dad. He got on well with his own parents. He always had a freshly-ironed shirt for Saturday night, always a good hot dinner waiting for him after work, and the old man could always be tapped for a quid or two towards the end of the week. He supposed his being an only child had a lot to do with it. After his older brother had been knocked down and killed by a car seven years ago, his parents had seemed to turn all their affection onto him. He didn't mind – he liked them.

He could always bring his mates round for a party, his father, would always chip in for the beer, his mother would always dance with the boys. The old man would even chat up the birds. No, they weren't like Gerry's parents. Miserable old sods.

His thoughts were interrupted by footsteps descending the long flight of stairs. A coloured station-worker came into view and walked towards the other end of the platform, entering a door marked "private".

Dave's thoughts returned to his present situation. Where's the bloody train? For once he'd got down there early only to be left hanging around in the gloom. Gerry would always come to the door with him to say goodnight, her passion becoming stronger as his thoughts of missing the last train became stronger. She'd finally let him go and wait at the door till he was out of sight.

He'd nonchalantly turn and wave back at her two or three times and she'd blow kisses but as soon as he turned the corner, he was off like a shot, his lungs soon sore with the sudden exertion of running. He invariably arrived at the station with a painful stitch in his side, dashed through the barrier without paying, took the stairs two or three at a time, and was usually just in time to leap through the closing doors of the train. It was a good thing Gerry never heard his curses if he wasn't in time. It meant a long walk home down the trouble-filled Commercial Road. There was nearly always a mob on some street corner, or a "perve" lingering in a doorway. Dave wasn't chicken but it *was* a drag.

Something moving caught his eye. A dark shape was moving along between the tracks. He walked to the edge of the platform and peered down the track into the gloom. Nothing. Then he noticed the shape had stopped. Realizing it must be a rat, he threw the empty milk carton to see if he could make it scamper back into the darkness of the tunnel, but it merely shrank beneath the electric rail. The boy looked up sharply as he heard noises coming from the dense black cave of the tunnel. It sounded like the rush of air, but not the sound caused by an approaching train. He glanced nervously back at the form lurking in beneath the track and up again as the noise grew louder. As he did, hundreds, it seemed, of small black bodies came pouring from the tunnel, some between the tracks, others up the ramp and along the platform.

He turned and ran even before he realized they were rats, much larger than normal, and much faster. He reached the stairs, a long, black river of vermin almost at his heels, and flew up them, three at a time. He slipped once, but quickly regained his balance, grasping at the hand-rail by the side, pulling at it to gain momentum. But a rat had raced ahead of him, and his next step was on its back, causing Dave to stumble once more. As his hand went to steady himself, sharp teeth snapped at his fingers. He shouted in fear, kicking out wildly, sending two of the bristling bodies back down over the backs of their companions. He lurched onwards, now weighed down by rats that had attached themselves to his clothes and his flesh. He fell again, hitting the bridge of his nose on the sharp corner of a step, causing blood to spill down his face and onto his white long-collared shirt.

He kicked and screamed but they pulled him back down the stairs, rolling to the bottom with him, ripping his body, shaking him as though he were a toy doll. His screams echoed through the old station. He half rose and before his senses blacked out completely he cried for his mother.

Errol Johnson pulled the door marked 'private' open and rushed out. He'd heard the screams and assumed someone had fallen down the long stairway to the platform. He knew it would happen someday – those stairs were too badly lit. If he ever became station-master, if coloureds ever became station-master's he'd clean it up and make it a respectable station. Just because it wasn't used by many people didn't mean it should be badly kept.

He stopped dead at the spectacle before him, his mouth hanging wide.

Millions of rats swarming all over the station. And big ones, like those he'd seen in his own country, but even bigger. His mind didn't even stop to evaluate. He ran, without looking back. There was only one place for him to go, the stairs being cut off by a struggling mass of vermin. Without hesitation, he ran down the ramp and into the dark womb of the tunnel. His fear drove him straight into the approaching train, mercifully killing before he was aware of death's presence.

The driver, who was braking anyway, slammed them on even harder, pitching his few passengers forward in their seats. As he emerged from the tunnel, the train's wheels screeching in high-pitched protest, the scene before him caused him to react instinctively, thereby saving the lives of his passengers and himself. He released the brakes and drove on.

The rats became still and glared at the huge intruding monster. Those beneath the tracks crouched low as it rumbled over them, the squealing from its wheels freezing them.

The passengers stared down through the window, horror-struck, wondering if the train had found its way down to the corridors of hell. One fell back as a dark furry body hurtled itself at him only to bounce off the window and back onto the platform. As the train began to gather speed, more of the creatures leapt at the windows, some falling between the train and the platform to be sliced by the grinding wheels. A rat broke through the window of one carriage and immediately attacked its solitary passenger. The man was strong and managed to pull the frenzied creature from his throat. It tore at his hands with teeth and claws, causing him to shout out in pain, but he still held its neck and body. His terror gave him added strength and speed; he threw it to the floor and brought

his heavy boot swiftly down on its head, crushing its skull. He
picked up the limp body, amazed at its size, and threw it
through the broken window into the black tunnel that the
train was now in. He sank into his seat, shock spreading
through his body, not knowing that within twenty-four hours
he would be dead.

The station-master choked on his tea as he heard screams
coming from the stairs. He spluttered as he tried to regain his
breath. Not another fight. Why was it that his station always
attracted hooligans on weekends? Especially Saturday nights.
Underground stations always attracted trouble on Saturday
nights from the yobbos and drunks, but Sundays usually
weren't too bad. He hoped that daft ape Errol wasn't involved. Always interfering. Making suggestions about how to
run the place. Helping drunks instead of booting them out.
Where did he think it was – Charing Cross?

Shadwell suited the station master. It was quiet compared
to most stations and that suited him fine. Of course it was
dirty, but what could you do with an old dump like this?
Anyway, it helped keep the people away.

When he'd recovered his composure, he slipped his jacket
on and stepped out from the ticket office. Without rushing he
ambled towards the top of the stairs to Platform One.

"What's going on down there?", he bellowed, squinting as
he tried to see through the dim lights. He heard one cry of
what sounded like, "Mum" and saw one black, thrashing shape.
He moved cautiously down a few steps and stopped again.
"Come on, who is it?"

The black shape seemed to break up into little shapes that
began mounting the stairs towards him. He heard a train
grinding to a halt downstairs, and then suddenly, for some
unknown reason, the whine of it picking up speed again and
carrying on through the station without stopping. Then he
heard the squeaks that sounded like hundreds of mice. He
realized that the creatures were coming up the stairs towards
him. Not mice – but rats. Horrible big rats. Black, ugly.

He moved surprisingly fast for a man of his bulk. He cleared
the few stairs he'd descended in two bounds and headed for
the ticket office, slamming the door behind him. He leaned

back against it for a couple of seconds, fighting for breath and giving his heartbeats a chance to slow down. He made for the 'phone and with trembling fingers dialled emergency.

"Police, Hurry! Police? This is Shadwell Underground, Stationmaster Green speak ..." He looked up as he heard a scuttling noise. Staring across at him from the ticket-office pay window was a huge, black, evil-looking rat.

He dropped the 'phone and ran to the back of the office. The windows were barred, preventing any escape. He looked around in desperation, his gross figure shaking with fear. He saw the cupboard set back in the wall, where brooms and buckets were kept for the cleaners, pulled it open and pushed himself inside, closing the door behind. He crouched, half sitting, whimpering, wetness spreading between his thighs, in the darkness, scarcely daring to breathe. That scream! It must have been Errol or someone waiting for a train. They'd got him and now they were coming for him! The driver of the train hadn't stopped. He'd see them and driven on. And there's no-one else on the station. Mother-of-God, what's that? Gnawing. Scraping. They're in the office. They're trying to eat their way through the cupboard door!

Chapter 10

Eight-thirty. The Monday morning rush was in full swing. The passengers on the underground train read their morning papers or novels; slept or dozed; chatted or thought; stood or sat. Some even laughed occasionally. Accountant clerks rubbed shoulders with financial directors; typists with models; tea-ladies with executives; filing clerks with computer programmers; black with white. The men stared boldly or secretly at the girls' legs; the girls stared back or pretended not to notice. Minds filled with the coming week; minds reflecting on the weekend past; minds almost blank.

Jenny Cooper sat reading the problems page of a women's magazine, occasionally smiling at the ridiculous situations some girls seemed to get themselves into. She scoffed at some of the answers too. Flicking over the page, not really interested in the words before her, her thoughts returned to the previous Saturday night and the party she'd gone to. She was impatient to get to work to tell her friends about the fabulous boy who'd taken her home – especially Marion, who always had hundreds of blokes and never let the other girls forget it. Jenny considered herself to be a little bit plain; her eyes were

too small and too close together, her nose just a fraction too
long. Her legs were good though; long, not too thin and not
to fat. Her hair always looked nice. Nice curls, nice soft
colour. And her face *was* quite attractive if she didn't smile
too broadly. Anyway, this boy really fancied her – he'd told
her. She'd had boyfriends but none of them up to Marion's
usual standard. She'd liked them but always felt slightly asha-
med of them when they'd taken her out. But this one was
different. He was just as good-looking as any of Marion's,
in fact, better than a lot of them. And he'd asked her out
again! Tonight. Pictures. She couldn't wait to show him off
to her friends – she'd make Marion green.

Violet Melray, sitting next to Jenny, read her historical
romance. She always became so engrossed in romantic fic-
tion, always knowing exactly how the heroine felt in every
situation, suffering with her, experiencing her disappoint-
ments, her happiness. She sighed inwardly as the hero, having
lost his wealth, his wife (who had been so wicked and conniving), and his right arm in a hunting accident, now returned to
the woman he really loved, the heroine, so soft, so pure, so
willing to have him back in her arms and comfort him in his
grief, ready to sacrifice everything for him, this man who had
betrayed her trust and who now needed her so much. Violet
remembered how romantic George had been. In their court-
ing days, he'd given her flowers, small gifts, little poems. How
thoughtful he'd always been. But now, sixteen years and three
kids later, he was more inclined to pat her back than tickle
her chin. He was a good man though, very straight, but very
soft.

He'd been a good husband to her and a good father to the
children, ever faithful, ever patient. Their love had mellowed
over the years, not really fading as most couple's seemed to.
But if only he wasn't so sensible. Every problem was tackled
with logic rather than emotion; and emotion was carefully
measured, never just let loose. If only once he would surprise
her. Do something startling. Not have an affair – but perhaps
flash his eyes at another woman. Or have a flutter on the
horses. Or come home drunk. Or punch his brother Albert on
the nose. But no, she wouldn't really change him. It wasn't his

fault that she had urges now and again for a bit of romantic adventure, a bit of glamour. At forty-two, she should have got over her wilder impulses for adventure. Now, with the kids at school and able to look after themselves, her only outlet was her part-time job in an insurance office. The men were pretty stodgy but some of the girls were a laugh. It kept her busy for most of the day anyway and she had enough to do when the kids got home from school and George from work. She reminded herself to go into Smith's at lunch-time for a new book.

Henry Sutton clung to his strap as the train lurched round a bend in the tunnel. He tried to read his folded paper but every time he attempted to open it out to turn a page, he nearly lost his balance. Eventually, he gave it up as a bad job and looked down at the woman sitting in front of him reading a book and wondered when it would be her station. No, she'd stay on for a while yet; the book-readers always had long journeys. The young girl next to her. No. Works in an office, won't get off until we reach the City or the West End, and it's only Stepney Green next stop. Over the years of rush-hour travel, Henry had become an expert on where people lived. It didn't work so well in the mornings – he rarely got a seat – but in the evenings, he would position himself in front of a person most likely to get off fairly soon. For instance: the scruffier the person, the sooner they reached their destination; coloured people never went further than West Ham; well-dressed people often changed at Mile End for the Central Line. Twenty years as a solicitor's clerk, mundane but comfortable, had taught him a lot about people too. Life proceeded at a steady, regular pace; not very exciting – the odd interesting scandal – but one day pretty much like another. No cases of murder, rape or blackmail – mainly divorce, embezzlement, or house purchasing. Steady stuff. Mostly monotonous, often dull. Secure. He was glad he wasn't married and able to lead his own life without worrying about children, schools, neighbours, H.P., holidays. Not that he really ever got up to much on his own. He believed in keeping himself to himself and not getting involved in other people's problems. He had enough of that at work, although he never became emotionally involved. The church choir was the only social outlet he enjoyed, meeting once a week to rehearse, and Sunday morning singing his heart out, the only form of exhibitionism he allowed himself.

He raised his glasses and rubbed the bridge of his nose. Mondays were neither depressing nor exhilarating for Henry Sutton; one day was much the same as any other.

The train suddenly gave a lurch and screeched to a halt, throwing the surprised solicitor's clerk onto the laps of Violet Melray and Jenny Cooper.

"Oh, excuse me" he stuttered, his face reddening as he pulled himself up again. Other passengers were in the same predicament and were now picking themselves up, some laughing, others tutting angrily.

"Here we go," a voice was heard to say. "Another twenty-minute delay." He was wrong. They sat or stood for forty minutes in a state of agitation, trying to hear the shouted conversation between the driver and the guard over their intercom. Henry Sutton, Violet Melray and Jenny Cropper were in the first carriage so they could hear the driver's replies to the guard's questions quite plainly. He'd seen something on the line, not quite sure what, but it had been quite large, so he'd jammed on his brakes and cut his power. Having decided that whatever it was man or animal, it must have been killed by the train and there wasn't much he could do about it now, so the obvious thing to do was to go on and send a crew back from the next station. The only trouble now was that he couldn't get any juice. No power. It could be that whatever he'd run over had done some damage to the train although he doubted it. A faulty cable maybe? He'd actually heard of rats chewing through cables.

The driver, or "motor-man" as he was officially called, had been on to central control and they'd advised him to sit tight for a while until they located and repaired the fault. But it was the smell of smoke that decided him upon his course of action. The passengers became aware of the smoke at the same time and began to stir apprehensively.

The next station, Stepney Green, wasn't very far, so he would get them off the train and up the tunnel. With so many passengers it would be dangerous, but it would be better than have them panic in the confined spaces of the carriages. Already he could hear excited voices coming from the carriage next door. He told us the guard of his intentions then opened the connecting door, to be confronted by anxious-looking faces.

"It's all right," he reassured them with false confidence. "Slight hitch, that's all. We're going to go along the tunnel to the next stop – it isn't far and the rails won't be live."

"But something's burning," a concerned-looking business-man informed him gruffly.

"That's all right, sir. No cause for alarm. We'll soon put that right." He made his way forward to the end of the carriage. "I'm just going to inform the rest of the passengers and then I'll be back to lead you through the tunnel." He disappeared into the adjoining compartment leaving the dismayed commuters in an uneasy silence.

A few minutes later, they heard a scream followed by shouts of alarm. The connecting door burst open and passengers spilled in, pushing and shoving their way through the crowded carriage. The smell of burning followed close behind. The hysteria spread like the fire that caused it.

Henry Sutton was once again thrown upon the two female travellers before him.

"Oh dear, oh dear," he murmured, his glasses skimming to the end of his nose. This time, the crush of people prevented him from disentangling himself from the frightened women. They were forced to stay locked together as men and women pushed by them, terrified now by the billowing smoke that began to fill the train. Scuffles broke out as men found their escape impeded by others. All the way down the tube train doors were being forced open and passengers were jumping down into the dark tunnel, some knocking themselves sense-less against the wall and being crushed by others landing on top of them.

Violet gasped for breath beneath the prostrate solicitor's clerk, while Jenny struggled to get free.

"I'm terribly sorry, ladies," he apologized, helpless to move. "If – if we keep calm, I'm sure the crush will ease soon and

then we'll be able to make our way off the train. I don't think
the fire will spread this way for a while. We've plenty of time."
Strangely enough, Henry felt extremely calm. For one whose
life had had so little adventure he marvelled at his own composure. He'd often wondered whether he'd be brave in time
of crisis and now, as people panicked, and pushed, and
screamed all around him, he'd surprised himself by his own
lack of fear. He felt quite pleased.

By now, the carriage was becoming less crowded as the
people used the side-doors to escape the choking smoke.

"Ah, now I think I can stand." Henry got to his feet and
reached down to pull the woman and the girl to theirs. "I
think we should stick together, ladies. When we get into the
tunnel we'll hold hands and feel out way along the wall. I'll
lead, come along."

He led the two white-faced passengers towards the front of
the carriage. Suddenly the screaming reached a new pitch. In
the gloom of the tunnel, lit by the lights of the train, they
could see struggling figures. There were so many faces out
there that they couldn't comprehend exactly what was happening. Henry caught a glimpse of one man, still wearing a
bowler-hat, disappearing from view beneath the window with
something black against his face. As they neared the open
door of the driver's compartment, they saw that people were
struggling to get back on the train but were being blocked by
those still trying to get off.

Henry and his two female companions reached the small
darkened driver's compartment.

"Now let me see," he said, half to himself, "there should be
a torch or a lantern somewhere here – ah, just the job." He
reached down for a long rubber-covered torch tucked away in
one corner. A sudden scraping noise made him turn towards
the driver's open door. Something black was crouched there.
He switched on the torch and shone a beam of light towards
it. Jenny screamed as it reflected on two shining, evil-looking
eyes. Instantly, without realizing his actions, Henry lashed out
with his foot, catching the rat's head and knocking it back
into the tunnel.

"It's one of those black rats that the papers were on

about!" Violet cried in horror. Jenny burst into tears, burying
her head into the older woman's shoulder. Henry shone the
torch down into the darkness and was dumb-struck at the
scene before him. In the confined space of the tunnel, men
and women were running, fighting, cowering as hundreds of
black rats rampaged amongst them, leaping and tearing, their
bloodlust stirring them into a frenzy. He quickly closed the
door and then looked back into the carriage. He saw that the
rats had entered the train and were now attacking the passengers who hadn't managed to get off or had scrambled back on.
He slammed the compartment door shut and switched off
his torch.

He was trembling slightly but managed to control the
tremor in his voice. "I think, our best bet is to sit tight for a
while, ladies."

They all jumped as something fell against the door. Jenny
began to moan loudly, her whole body shaking fitfully. Violet
did her best to comfort her. "It's all right, dear. They can't
get in here," she soothed.

"But you must keep quiet," Henry said, placing a hand
kindly on her shoulder. "They mustn't hear us. I think I broke
that devil's neck, so he won't try to get in. I suggest we all
crouch down on the floor and keep as still as possible." He
helped lower the sobbing girl to a sitting position and took
one more glance out of the window. He wished he hadn't.
His mind registered a mental picture he knew he would never
forget for as long as – he quickly pushed the thought of life
and death from his mind. Below him was part of a nightmare.
A scene from hell. He saw bloody-covered limbs; torn faces;
ripped bodies. A man stood almost opposite him, against the
wall, stiff and straight, his eyes lifelessly staring, it seemed,
into his own, while three or four rats gorged themselves on his
bare legs. A fat woman, completely naked cried pitifully as
she beat at two rats clinging to her ample breasts. A young
boy of about eighteen was trying to climb to the top of the
train by pushing his feet against the wall and slowly levering
himself up. A huge rat ran up the side of the wall and landed
on his lap, causing the boy to fall back onto the ground.
Screams pervaded the air. Cries for help beat into his brain.

All in the half-gloom, against the blackness of the tunnel, as though the whole event was taking place in black limbo. And everywhere scurrying, furry black creatures, running up the walls, launching themselves into the air, only stopping when their victims' struggles ceased, and then eating and drinking.

Henry sank to his knees and weakly crossed himself.

He jumped when a hand touched his shoulder. "What should we do?" Violet asked him, trying to see his face in the darkness. He made an effort to push the horrible scene from his mind.

"We'll wait for a while – see what happens. They're bound to send someone down the tunnel to investigate. Shouldn't be too long." He reached out for Violet's hand and patted it softly. He began to secretly enjoy the woman's dependence on him. In the past, he'd always been a little shy of the opposite sex, but now, amidst the chaos, he was finding a new side to his timid nature. Sense of pride in himself began to quell the fear inside.

Abruptly, the screaming ceased. They didn't move for a few seconds, their ears straining for the slightest sound. And then they heard moaning. It started with one long low moan and developed into several more. Soon the whole tunnel echoed with cries of misery, wailing voices, calls for help. But there were no more screams. The strident urgency had gone from the voices. It was as though the mutilated people – those left alive – knew that nothing more could happen to them. The horror had been perpetrated, now they could only live or die.

Henry raised himself and looked through the window. He could see one or two bodies nearby, but the blackness concealed anything else.

"I think they've gone." He turned back to the woman and girl. "There doesn't seem to be any sign of them."

Violet got to her knees and peered out. "But – but what's that glow. There's a red glow coming from somewhere."

Henry leapt to his feet. "Of course. The fire! It's spreading, and probably frightened off the rats. We'll have to get out."

"No," cried Jenny. "We can't go out there. They'll be waiting!"

"And we can't stay here," he told her, not unkindly. "Look, I think they've gone now, frightened by the fire. I'll go out and look first and find out. Then I'll come back for you."

"Don't leave us." Violet clutched at his arm. He smiled at her, his face now visible in the red glow. She was a fine-looking woman, he thought. Probably married. Kids too. Wouldn't look at me twice at a more normal time. Pity.

"All right. We'll go together."

"No, no, I'm not going out there." Jenny crouched back against the opposite corner.

"You must, my dear. You'll suffocate here before very long." The smoke had begun to get heavier. "It'll be safe now – you'll see." He reached out for her and forced her to her feet, Violet helping him. "When we get out, I don't want either of you to look round," he told them. "Just hold onto me and look straight ahead. And please trust me."

Cautiously opening the door he shone his torch along the tunnel, although he hardly needed it now because of the glow from the fire somewhere back along the train. Bodies were strewn all along the track as far as he could see, some amongst them still moving, some crawling up the tunnel, away from the carriage, others lying perfectly still. He thought he saw small shapes moving against them but wasn't sure whether it wasn't the flickering light deceiving his eyes.

"Come along, ladies. Remember what I said and keep your eyes straight ahead – we mustn't stop for anything – or anybody." Normally a compassionate man, he knew it would be fatal to try and help any of the injured. They would have to be rescued later.

He climbed down and reached up to help the young girl, who was shaking uncontrollably. He talked to her softly, coaxing her, trying to soothe her distraught nerves. Violet smiled down at him, frightened, but placing her life in this kind little man's hands. They went forward, bending to escape the smokey upper air. Henry first, the girl next with her face against his back, Violet following up close behind her arms around Jenny.

They stumbled forward, trying to ignore the moans, the feeble cries for help. Henry felt a hand weakly grasp his trou-

sers but it fell away at his next step. He knew he couldn't stop,
the lives of the woman and the girl depended on him. He
would come back with the rescuers. His duty now was to get
the three of them out, to warn the people at the station ahead.
He heard a squeal and felt something soft squirm beneath his
feet. Shining the torch down he discovered a rat glaring up at
him. He saw others all round – but these were different from
others he'd seen. They were smaller. Normal. Hideous – but
normal. He kicked out at it and it scampered away as another
dashed forward and bit into Henry's trouser leg.

Fortunately, it only tore into the material and he was able
to bring his leg up swiftly against the wall, causing the rat to
lose its grip and fall to the ground. He brought his foot down
hard on its back and was shocked to hear the crunch of small
bones breaking.

Jenny screamed.

"It's all right, it's all right," he said quickly. "They're ordinary rats. They're dangerous, but nothing like the big ones.
They'll probably be more frightened of us than we are of
them."

Through her fear, Violet felt admiration well up inside her
for the little man. She'd hardly noticed him on the train, of
course. He was the type you didn't really see. Just a face. The
sort of man you would never speculate about – just wouldn't
arouse the interest. But now, down here in this frightful
place, how brave he was. Rescuing her from this carnage. Her
and the girl of course. But how brave!

When Henry had killed the rat, Jenny had been forced to
look around her. The sight caused her to retch. She sagged
against the wall, wanting to collapse but being held by the
woman behind her. Why wouldn't the man let them get back
on the train where they'd been safe? She tried to stagger back
but Henry caught her arm.

"This way, dear. It won't take long."

As they stumbled on, they saw rats feeding on the corpses
of men and women – people who had set out to work, thinking it would be the usual Monday, minds filled with small
worries and small joys, never expecting to die that day. Never
expecting to die at any time in such a gruesome way. The three

went on, choking with the smoke, now and again falling to be picked up by the others, moving all the time, finally leaving the dead or maimed behind. Suddenly, Henry stopped, causing Jenny and Violet to bump into him.

"What is it?" asked the older woman anxiously.

"Just ahead. There's something there. I saw a gleam." He followed a silver rail with his torch-beam until it fell upon four black objects. Four giant rats. Waiting for them. Lurking in the dark, waiting for them. Neither party moved for a few frozen seconds, then the human trio began to slowly back away. The rats just stared. Henry heard Violet gasp behind him and her grip tightened on his arm. "Behind us. There's more," she managed to say.

He whirled around and saw them. Two. Advancing stealthily towards them. He realised they were trapped. Now the four in front had begun to move forward, taking tiny crouching steps, the back muscles tensing, ready to spring. Perhaps I could make it on my own, he thought. Jump over the ones ahead and keep running. The girl and the woman would never make it – but on my own there might be a chance.

"Against the wall, ladies." He pushed them back, shutting out thoughts of escape from his mind. "Keep behind and if they try to get past me, kick out, hard as you can." He took off his jacket and wrapped it round his arm keeping the light from the torch on the rats now gathered before him. The girl hid her face against the wall, the woman began to weep for her children.

One rat moved forward, its chill gaze never leaving Henry's eyes.

A light flashed from ahead in the tunnel. They heard voices. Footsteps. More lights. The whole tunnel lit up as the footsteps and voices grew louder.

The rats and the three people looked towards the sounds, neither group stirring. Scuffling noises brought Henry's eyes back to the rats in time to see them disappear towards the burning train. All except one. The one that had been closest was still there, studying the man. Not moving, seemingly unafraid. The solicitors clerk felt icy cold as though his very soul was being scrutinized. He became paralysed with fear. Almost contemptuously, the large rat turned its head towards the approaching men, looked once again at Henry, and then fled.

"Over here, over here" Henry called.

Soon they were surrounded by uniformed men; police and underground staff. As Henry told them of the appalling events, they stared in disbelief.

"Come along, sir. Rats couldn't — and wouldn't — attack a whole train-load of people," a police sergeant said, shaking his head. "Giant or not, they couldn't get into a train. Perhaps it's the fumes, sir. They've made you a bit muddled."

Violet Melray pushed roughly past the little clerk and shouted angrily. "Well go and bloody look then!" and turned back, taking his hand into hers, said more softly, "Thank you. Thank you for helping us."

Henry blushed and dropped his gaze.

"Er, yes, well," the sergeant said, we'll go on. Two of my men will take you on to the station."

"No, Henry said, "I'll come back to the train with you. You'll need all the help you can get." He looked at the woman still clutching his hand. "Goodbye. I'll see you again."

Before he could pull his hand away, she stepped forward and kissed his cheek.

"Goodbye," she whispered.

Chapter 11

Harris felt happy as he walked into the noisy classroom. The weekend had done him the world of good. Must do it more often. Fresh air, open spaces. Green. Can't beat it.

"All right, you lot, shut up!" he barked above the din. "Scalley, sit down and blow your nose. Thomas, away from the window, back to your seat. Maureen, put your mirror away now. Right. All had a good weekend? That's enough! Let's call the register."

The pupils sensed he was in a good mood and knew they could get away with a little more cheek than usual. This morning, anyway.

"Only two absentees. Not bad for a Monday morning. Yes, Carlos, what is it? Toilet? But you've only just got in. Go on then, you'll never concentrate if you don't."

Carlos, a thin dark-skinned boy, thanked-him-sir, and left the room, a smirk on his face when his back was to the teacher.

"Carol, give out the paper – Shelagh, give out the pencils. We're going to draw some animals today," Harris told the class.

"Can I draw a pig, sir?" a boy at the back asked.

"Why a pig, Morris?"

"I can copy tubby Toomey, sir."

The offended fat boy swivelled round in his chair as the class erupted into laughter and swore at his tormentor.

"Come out here, Morris," Harris said, firm-mouthed. The boy slouched to the front of the class. "Any good at drawing monkeys, Morris?"

"No, sir."

"Well try copying from a mirror," Harris told him knowing the class expected and enjoyed his bringing-down of a loud-mouth, even though any one of them could be next. Feeble, Harris thought, but not bad for a Monday morning. "Right, get on with it. Any animal you like, but I don't want any to look like me. When you've finished, we'll choose the best one, then I'll explain why it's the best one. Remember your light and shade." He walked up and down the aisles, talking to them individually, giving answers, posing questions. He came to a boy named Barney, small for his fourteen years, but very bright, good at drawing but still needing to learn the techniques of painting. He was especially good with pen and ink, a skill he'd taught himself by copying comic books. Harris looked over the boy's shoulder and stared at the picture taking form.

"What made you draw a rat, Barney?" he asked.

"Dunno, sir," Barney said, sucking the end of his pen, then adding, "Saw one the other day. Big one, like Keogh saw . . ." His voice trailed off as he remembered his classmate who was now dead. The rest of the class became silent at the mention of Keogh's name.

"Whereabouts?" asked the teacher.

"By the canal. Tomlins Terrace."

"Did you see where it went?"

"It jumped over a wall and disappeared into the bushes."

"What bushes? There isn't a park down there."

"Where the lock-keeper used to live. It's like a jungle now the canal's been shut down."

Harris vaguely remembered the old house that stood well back from the road, where, as a kid, he used to go to watch the barges passing through the lock. The lock-keeper liked the kids to watch him work provided they weren't cheeky, and used to encourage them to come. Funny, he'd forgotten all about the place. He'd been down Tomlins Terrace a few times recently and hadn't remembered the house had been there. It must have been because of the "jungle" in front.

"Did you tell the police?" he asked the boy.

"Nah." Barney turned his attention back to his drawing adding a few more strokes to his strikingly evil-looking rat.

Might have known, Harris thought to himself. Kids around this area don't get involved with the law through choice.

At that moment, Carlos burst into the room in a state of extreme agitation.

"Sir, sir, in the playground! There's one of them things!" He gesticulated towards the window, his eyes wide, smiling in his excitement.

The whole class rushed as one towards the windows.

"Back to your seats!" Harris roared, and strode quickly to a window. He drew in a sharp breath at what he saw.

There wasn't "one of them things" but several. As he watched, more joined the first bunch. Huge black rats. *The* rats. They crouched in the playground, staring at the school building. More, then more.

"Close all windows," he ordered, quietly. "Johnson, Barney, Smith; go round to all the other classrooms and ask the teachers to close all windows. Scalley, go to the Headmaster's study and ask him to look out of his window – no, I'd better go." If a boy went, the Headmaster would probably think it was some kind of prank, and valuable seconds would be wasted. "I don't want anybody to move from this room. And no noise. Cutts, you're in charge." The tallest boy in the class stood up. The boys were excited now, the girls becoming more and more nervous.

He hurried out of the room and made towards the Principal's study. As he walked down the corridor, several of the teachers' heads popped out of various doors.

"What's going on?" he was asked nervously by Ainsley, one of the old-timers of the school.

He told him quickly and hurried on. There was a strange hush throughout the school, a hush that could be entirely ruined if only one girl became hysterical.

Barney dashed from one of the classrooms.

Harris caught his arm and told him: "Steady, Barney. Take it slowly and calmly. Don't frighten the girls. We don't want panic, do we?"

"No, sir," was the breathless reply.

As Harris approached the stairs leading up to the next floor and the Headmaster's study, he looked down the short flight to the main doors. Naturally, they were open.

He crept slowly down, his hand on the rail to steady himself. As he reached the bottom, he heard a soft noise on the stone steps outside. Springing quietly to the side of the double-doors he glanced out, ready to slam both sides shut instantaneously. On the wider top step he saw a small boy looking back into the playground where about thirty of the rodents had now gathered.

Jesus Christ, Harris thought in horror. He must have walked right past them!

He stepped outside and swiftly scooping the small boy up, dashed back into the building. He dumped him on the floor without ceremony and turned back to close the doors. The rats hadn't stirred. He shut the heavy doors quickly but quietly and bolted them, then breathed out for the first time in nearly two minutes.

"There's animals in the playground, sir," the seven-year-old boy told him with wide eyes, but no trace of fear. "What are they? What are they doing there, sir?"

Ignoring the question because he didn't know what to tell him, Harris picked the boy up and raced back up the stairs. Putting him down at the top he told him to run along to his classroom. He heard the murmur of voices as teachers began to gather in the corridor. He ran up the next flight of stairs, three at a time, and almost collided with the Headmaster as he emerged from his office.

"Please 'phone the police, Mr. Norton." Harris said urgently. "I'm afraid we've got trouble."

"I already have, Mr. Harris. Have you seen what's in the playground?"

"Yes – that's the trouble I mean. They're the giant ones, the killers."

They went back into the study and looked out of the window. The rats had multiplied it seemed to a couple of hundred.

"The playground's black with them," the young teacher said in disbelief.

"What do they want?" The Headmaster looked at Harris as though he would know.

"The children," said Harris.

"It won't take the police long to get here – but what they'll do about the situation is another matter. Let's make sure every door and window is shut tight. All the children must go up to the top floor and barricade themselves in. I still don't quite believe it's happening but let's not waste any time on pondering over the situation." The Headmaster strode briskly to the door.

"Now you check every possible opening, Mr. Harris, I'll get the staff organised."

Harris followed the gaunt figure of the Headmaster down the stairs where the buzz of conversation was beginning to build up. He heard him clap his hands and order silence. Harris brushed past the throng of teachers, looking into every room, making sure all the windows were firmly closed.

Thank God all the lower windows had iron grilles over them to prevent broken window panes from boisterously kicked footballs. Good.

All seemed tight. Now the staffroom.

As he entered he saw one of the windows was open, and because it faced the narrow passage between the building and the outer wall, it had no grille to protect it. And on the floor before it, sat one of the creatures.

How it had scaled the wall was something Harris would never know, but there it was, as though it were a scouting party for the others. It looked to and fro, sniffing the air, its pointed nose twitching. It saw Harris and rose on its haunches. It stood at least two feet from the ground. The teacher stepped inside and slammed the door behind him. He had to close that window.

This particular rat spent no time studying its victim – it

sprang forward, straight off its haunches and into the air, aiming itself for Harris's throat. But the teacher was just as fast. He reached for a chair even as the creature's muscles tensed for the leap and swung it before him. The chair struck the rat's body in mid-jump, like a cricket bat meeting a ball, and threw it to one side, the wood splintering.

The rat landed on its feet and sprang towards Harris again, who brought the chair crashing down on its back. It was stunned for a few seconds, but still not severely hurt. However, it had gained the teacher time enough to reach for the heavy poker lying in the hearth of the unlit fire. He brought it down viciously, more in hate than fear, on the rat's thin skull with a sickening thud. Then again. And again. He turned towards the window in time to see another claw its way onto the sill. Without hesitation, he lashed out with the poker, knocking the rat back down into the narrow passageway below. He pulled the window shut and leaned against it, gasping for breath and trying to control his trembling knees. The window was a type with fine wire mesh set in the glass to prevent it shattering.

"It *should* hold them," he said aloud.

Then he went to the staffroom door, took the key from the inside, stepped out and locked it. But not before taking a close look at the creature lying on the threadbare carpet.

Its body must have been at least two feet long, its tail another nine or ten inches. The bristly fur wasn't exactly black, but very dark brown, with lots of black speckles mottling it. Its head was larger in proportion to the ordinary rodent's and its incisors were long and pointed. Its half-lidded eyes had the lifeless glaze of the dead, but its partially-covered teeth seemed to grin wickedly. Even in death, the body seemed deadly, as though the disease it bore could be passed on by mere touch.

Once outside in the hall, Harris saw that the children were being herded towards the stairs.

"Are you all right, Mr. Harris?" the Headmaster came striding towards him.

"Yes. I've killed one of the monsters." Harris realized he still held the blood-stained poker.

"Good man. Well, the place is sealed off and the police will soon be here, so I don't think we've anything to worry about," the Headmaster said reassuringly, his smile disappearing instantly at Harris's next remark: "What about the basement?"

They both turned towards the cellar stairs and broke into a run as they neared them. They stopped at the top and peered down into the gloom.

"I think we'll be all right," said the Headmaster. "Mr. Jenkins, the caretaker, will probably be down there checking the boiler. It always takes him a while to get it going on Monday mornings. Heaven knows, I've complained about the cold water on Mondays enough..." he broke off, slightly annoyed at the young teacher who had carried on down apparently not listening to a word he was saying.

Harris approached the door of the basement with some caution, pressed his ear to it, and listened. He shushed the Headmaster with a finger to his mouth as the older man reached him.

"Oh, come along, man" the Headmaster pushed by him impatiently, and grasping the handle, swinging the door open wide. "Jenkins, are you...." his words choked off at the sight that met his eyes.

Black, scurrying creatures, swarming all around the basement. A small, high window, level with the playground outside, was wide open, and in poured more and more of the furry beasts, a constant stream of vermin.

And they were feeding on something on the floor. All Harris and the Headmaster were able to see was a single boot, protruding from the writhing mass of bodies. The teacher pulled his Principal back from the open doorway as several dark shapes dashed forward. He grabbed the handle and pulled hard but two of the rats slithered through, a third being trapped by its shoulder. He kicked at it three times before it fell back into the basement. He whirled around to see the other two scampering up the stairs. The Headmaster was on his knees staring after them.

"My God, they're enormous," was all he could utter.

"If they reach the children...:" Harris began to say.

"I'll stop them, I'll stop them, Harris, you cover that door.

Block it with anything you can find. It's extremely heavy, but we want to be sure!" The distressed Headmaster was regathering his wits. "When you've done that, come straight upstairs."

"Right, but don't let them bite you!" Harris shouted after the ascending figure, "Their bite's fatal. Keep them away from you."

He looked around for something big to block the door with. The store-room was on his right. He opened it and carefully looked in. No windows, so it should be all right. He switched on the light. Tables, chairs, blackboards. Good. He pulled out a heavy table and turned it on its side, then pulled it along to the basement door. He upended it and was pleased to discover that it completely covered the door. He pushed it flush against it and went back to the store-room. He noticed an old radiator leaning against the wall and dragged it out, making a loud grating noise on the floor. He leaned it against the upturned table and went back for some chairs.

Just then, he heard a scream from upstairs. He picked up the discarded poker and raced upstairs.

The Headmaster was on the floor of the corridor, struggling with the two hideous rats. Mercifully, the door at the end of the corridor had been closed, and the children had all escaped to the floor above. The Headmaster had one of the rats by the throat and was fighting to keep it from his face. The other was boring a hole in his side.

"Help me, help me!" he implored Harris, turning his head to see the teacher.

Sickened, knowing his Principal was already dead, Harris ran forward and brought the poker down with all his might on one of the rats. It squealed, high-pitched, an octave above a frightened child's, and withdrew its teeth from the struggling man's side. Its back was broken, but it made an attempt to crawl towards Harris. He brought his foot down on its head and crushed it. He couldn't hit the second rat for fear of hurting the Headmaster, so he dropped the poker and reached for it with his hands. He grabbed it near its shoulders and lifted, taking care not to let its snapping teeth touch his body. Unfortunately, the Headmaster was too frightened to loose his grip on the squirming rodent.

"Let go, let go!" Harris shouted, now lifting the man with the rat.

But the Headmaster was too crazed with terror to hear. The teacher braced his foot against the Headmaster's chest and pushed him back to the floor, staggering back as the grip was released and falling, but still holding the rat high. Its weight and its strength were tremendous, and he felt his jacket and shirt being torn to shreds by the clawing feet. Holding it from behind, he raised himself to one knee and pushed it against the floor. He saw the Headmaster crawling away from him, his eyes never leaving the squirming monster in his grasp, backing away towards the wall, trying to push himself into it. In the background, Harris could hear the sound of police sirens. Where the hell have they been? What am I going to do with this?

He looked around desperately. The thing was slipping from his grip. He wouldn't be able to hold on much longer. And one bite from those teeth, even if he killed the bloody thing, one bite and he'd die later. 3c had an aquarium. That was the answer. He'd drown it. But all the doors were bloody shut. He could never hold on with one hand.

"Mr. Norton," he shouted. "The door to 3c! Open it, quick, I can't hold on much longer!"

The Headmaster shook his head, dully, never taking his gaze from the rat.

"Open that fucking door!" Harris screamed.

The elder man at last tore his eyes away from the rat and looked at the red-faced teacher. He nodded slowly and began to crawl towards 3c's classroom.

"Hurry, hurry," Harris shouted

In what seemed an eternity, the Headmaster reached the door and lifted a shaky, blood-soaked hand towards the handle. The blood made his hand too slippery to turn it and he had to reach up with his other. At last, the door opened.

Harris dragged the rat along the ground, his fingers aching, trying to squeeze the life out of the wriggling body, but not having the strength or the grip. The rat dug its claws into the wooden floor, forcing him to hold its head and shoulders slightly off the floor. The small head snapped from side to side, endeavouring to sink its teeth into the man's flesh. But Harris was careful, so very careful. When he got to the door, the Headmaster uttered a small cry and kicked out, catching his leg and almost causing him to lose his grip.

"Get out of the way," he said slowly, through clenched teeth. "Get out of the fucking way!" Louder.

The Headmaster scrambled aside and Harris was in. He saw the tank on the window-sill. He moved towards it. When he came to the teacher's desk at the head of the class, he swung the rat up onto it, using all his strength, but never loosening his grip. Then he pushed the desk forward with his body towards the aquarium, holding the rat's head against the table, his body being raked by the creature's hind-legs.

At last, the desk butted against the window-sill. He raised one leg and crawled on top of it, then dragged the rat towards the tank full of water.

He rested before he made the final effort. Gathering all his strength, sweat streaming from his face, he raised himself and the rat and plunged the writhing body into the water.

The tank seemed to explode. Water and fish cascaded over him but he held on grimly pushing its head down to the deep bottom, ignoring the pain in his chest and arms. He began to wonder if there would be enough water left in the tank to drown the rat, or whether its flying limbs would crack the glass sides. But gradually, the struggles became weaker, the twists of its body more feeble, the jerk of its head less violent. Finally, there was no movement at all. But Harris still held it there. Just to be sure.

He looked up, through the window. Several police cars had arrived, and many blue-uniformed men stood outside the front gate, not knowing what to do.

He finally released the dead body and wearily climbed off the table. His clothes were torn, and blood covered his shirt-front, but he was fairly sure he hadn't been bitten. He walked back to the Headmaster, who was still sitting in the doorway with his head in his hands.

"It's all right now, sir. The police are here. They'll soon clear them." Harris knelt down beside the trembling man.

"It was horrible," the Headmaster said, raising his head from his hands. "Frightful. Those foul creatures were waiting for me. They weren't running away at all. They were at the top waiting for me."

Harris didn't know what to say. How could you comfort someone you knew was going to die within twenty-four hours?

"Let's go upstairs, sir. We'll be safer there." He helped the Headmaster to his feet. They walked down the corridor towards the door leading to the stairs.

When Harris tried to open it, he found it was locked.

"Come on, they can't turn bloody door-knobs, you know!" he shouted, banging on the door with his fist.

They heard the sound of footsteps and then bolts drawn back.

"I'm so sorry, we didn't realise anybody else was still down here," Ainsley apologized, his bald head peeping round the door. "Oh, dear, is everything all right?" he asked, anxiously looking at their bloodied clothes.

They half-carried the Headmaster through, closing the door behind them.

"Are the children okay?" Harris asked.

"The girls are beginning to get a bit hysterical, but the boys still have plenty of swagger in them," replied Ainsley, catching his breath under the weight of the Headmaster.

"They'll need it," muttered Harris.

They took the injured Headmaster to his study and laid him in his armchair.

"I'll be all right now. Go and see to the children." His face was pale, and Harris wondered if it was imagination or could he actually detect a tinge of yellow in the injured man's face? And did the skin really look tight or was it just the stiffness of pain?

"Mr. Ainsley will treat your cuts, sir," he said. "I'll go and find out what's happening."

He left the study, feeling pity for the man he'd never liked, but had at least respected. The sight of him grovelling on the floor like a frightened child would stay in his mind for a long time.

He entered a classroom full of teachers and children and all heads turned towards him. He noticed the door to the adjoining room was open and anxious faces peering in. He beckoned the teachers to gather round him.

"The Headmaster's been injured," he said quietly, so the children wouldn't hear. "I think we'll be safe enough up here, but we'll barricade the doors just in case the rats get up the stairs. Get all the girls in one corner and away from the windows. The bigger boys can help push the desks and chairs against the door."

Grimble, a beak-nosed, sparrow of a man, pushed forward. "Really, as Deputy-Head, I. . . ." he began.

"We've no time for internal politics now, Grimble" Harris snapped, making some of the younger teachers hide smiles of pleasure behind their hands. Grimble was well-known and disliked for his conniving and petty ways. He turned away, huffily.

Harris went over to a window and opened it. He saw many police cars, among them a van-load of dogs. Some of the police were donning protective clothing. Two fire-engines rounded the corner at the end of the road, their frantic sirens adding to the noise. Crowds had gathered in the narrow street.

Below, he saw that the number of rats had thinned out considerably. Then he discovered why. They were disappearing two or three abreast through the small ground-level window to the boiler-room. Others were making for the narrow passageway at the side of the building. He assumed the staff-room window was their target.

He heard screaming behind him. Turning, he found one of the girls had become hysterical and was sitting at a desk while some of her classmates and one of the women teachers tried to comfort her.

A voice hailed him through a loudspeaker, sounding mechanical, inhuman: "Are you all right up there? Is anybody injured?"

Harris cupped his hands around his mouth and shouted: "Yes, we're okay so far. One man injured though!"

"Right. Well, barricade yourselves in. We don't know what the rats are up to yet, but they may try to reach you."

Of course they'll try to bloody reach us, Harris thought to himself. What does he think they're here for? A school outing? He fumed impatiently as the policeman turned and waved his arms at the squad cars, instructing them to clear the way for the fire-engines.

He turned back to the school and raised the loudspeaker again: "We're going to set the dogs on them first, and while they're occupied we'll try to reach you with ladders from the fire-engines." He obviously knew of the lethal bite of the vermin and wasn't going to risk his men against them.

"No!" Harris shouted back. "You'll never get all these children down those ladders. And your dogs won't last five minutes against those rats!"

"Do not panic up there. I repeat: do not panic. The experts will soon be here."

Harris swore under his breath as the voice droned on: "We believe they are bringing gas to deal with the problem. Please keep calm. They will not be very long."

The teacher groaned aloud. How long would it take those monsters to gnaw their way through a door? They weren't ordinary rats; they had intelligence, system. It would only take one of those monsters to get through to create havoc amongst these kids.

"Listen," he called out again. "The hoses! Flood the basement! Flood the lower classrooms! At least it'll panic them!"

He saw the policeman, whom he assumed was a Chief-Inspector conferring with a fireman. The firemen suddenly burst into activity, and began unwinding the long, thick hoses. Meanwhile the dogs were yelping excitedly, straining at their leashes, eager to tackle the black creatures. Two burst loose and streaked across the playground towards the thronging rats. The first, a hefty Alsatian, picked up one of the rats by the neck, shook it violently, and threw it into the air. The second dog, a massive Dobermann leapt into the thick of the furry mass, snapping its huge jaws in all directions.

But they were soon covered by the rodents, being pulled down, their coats covered in blood. Several times they rose, but always they were dragged back to the ground. The other dogs were turned loose, about ten of them, and they flew into the melée. One actually trampled over the backs of the rats and scrambled through the small basement window.

Harris, watching from above, shuddered at the thought of its fate.

Although the dogs were brave, they were no match for the vast number of giant rats. Soon they were either lying on the ground being torn apart or trying to hobble back to their grief-stricken trainers. The men themselves had to be ordered back by their Chief-Inspector. He alone amongst them knew the risk involved, of the deadly disease carried by the vermin, and had no intention of allowing his men to lay down their lives until it was entirely essential for the sake of the children.

Suddenly, the hoses came into action. They swept through the playground, icy torrents of water, clearing a path clean through the rats, tossing them against the brick wall of the school building. They scampered in all directions, scrambling over each others backs, fighting amongst themselves to get away. The blood from the dogs was soon washed away by the steady flow of water.

A jet was aimed at the basement window, pushing several rats inside but preventing any more from entering.

The children, who had by now crowded round the windows, cheered at the sight of the disrupted vermin. As the rats began to disperse, most running towards the coal bunkers, another jet of water was directed at the downstairs windows. The crash of glass as it showered into the classrooms brought grins of delight to many of the pupils.

Harris turned away from the window and walked across the room, gently pushing his way through the throng of children.

"Where's the Headmaster?" he asked Grimble.

"You should know. He was with you," was the curt reply.

"Pull some of these desks back. He must still be in his study with Ainsley."

The desks were pulled back allowing him just enough room to open the door and slip through.

"I'm going to see if they're okay, then I'll check the doors in the corridor," he said. "Push the barricade back after me.

If I come back fast and bang on the door, tell them to get those ladders up here. But don't open the door – I'll go into the Headmaster's study and get away from that window."

He closed the door behind him and heard the grating of the desks being pushed against it. He noticed the door of the Headmaster's room was wide open. Hurrying to it he breathed a sigh of relief when he found old Ainsley still fussing over the injured Principal.

"He – he seems fine now, Harris," Ainsley said, mopping the Headmaster's face with a wet flannel.

"Good. I'm going to check all the doors now and I want you to shut this one after me. Stay here, and if there's more trouble. . . ." he paused, not bothering to explain what he meant by "more trouble," but letting the silence do it for him. "If there's more trouble, go to the windows and call to the firemen. They'll get a ladder up to you." He didn't suggest they join the others in the classrooms – the sight of the blood-soaked Headmaster would frighten them too much. Up to now, the children had been remarkably controlled, but the sight of blood could easily push them over the edge.

He closed the door and walked quickly to the stairs. He opened the door fractionally and peeped through. All clear. Good. He went through, closed it, and crept down the stairs. Water was seeping underneath the door at the bottom. He opened it cautiously. The corridor was empty of life. One of the dead rats that had attacked the Headmaster lay in the water. For a moment, Harris thought he saw it move, but realised its body was merely being stirred by the surging water.

He splashed down the corridor, remembering to close the door behind him but opening all the classroom doors to allow the water to flow more freely. He passed the staffroom and thought he heard noises. The basement was the more urgent problem at the moment. That was where he'd seen most of the rats disappear. He had to make sure the door was still firm, maybe shove some more furniture against it. He could come back and deal with the staffroom door later.

He descended the stairs to the basement, taking care not to slip in the gushing water. He suspected more fire-engines had arrived and the forces outside were using more hoses to completely flood the lower floors.

He reached the bottom and waded towards the door. He could hear frantic scraping, scratching. He leaned forward to listen more intently above the noise of the swirling water. Yes, they were trying to scrape their way through the door. He eased the desk back slightly to see what damage they'd done. Christ, cracks were beginning to appear already. He could hear them gnawing at the wood now. Dropping the desk back he plodded to the storeroom. He looked around. Just the thing, heavy drapes. Old curtains that had been used in the school hall. He dragged them down from the shelf where they'd laid for the best part of a year, ready to be used for the next end-of-term prize-giving. They were heavy, but one would be enough for his purpose.

He left them draped over a bench, to prevent them getting wet and thus heavier, and went to a stack of blackboards. They were of the old type – they had to be used with easels – and took two. Carrying them outside, he leaned them against the wall. Then he pulled the radiator and the desk back away from the basement door.

He saw bulges in the wood where the rats had nearly eaten their way through. God, they must have strength in those jaws! Quickly he went back to the store-room and gathered up the curtain. He hurried back in time to see the wood beginning to splinter.

Almost in a panic, he stuffed the material in the crack beneath the door, folding it to make as many layers as possible. He grabbed the blackboards and slid them up against the door, as close to the bottom as the curtain would allow. Then he pushed the table up against the door, and the radiator against that, re-enforcing the barricade with chairs and boxes – anything he could find from the store-room.

At last satisfied, he leaned back against the wall and regained his breath. He thought he could hear squeals from inside but wasn't sure if it was his mind playing tricks on him.

By now he was knee-deep in water. He waded to the stairs and climbed up. As he gained the top step he heard a cracking noise coming from the staffroom door. He saw a long black pointed head emerging, still gnawing at the surrounding wood. He stood frozen to the spot. Would it never end? He looked around desperately and caught sight of the heavy poker he'd used before, still lying in the corridor, almost hidden by the streaming water. He sprang forward, slipped in the wet and fell headlong. Glancing back, he saw the rat's shoulders emerge from the widening hole. Frantically, he stumbled forward on all fours, snatched for the poker and got to his feet, using the wall to steady himself.

It was almost as though the rat knew of his intention as it redoubled its attempt to escape from the splintered wood. Most of its body was out, only its heavy flanks holding it captive.

Harris ran forward, this time taking care not to fall. Without pause, he brought the weapon down upon the twisting skull. Amazingly, it missed as the rat pulled its head to one side, and crashed against the door-frame. The rat bared its large, sharp teeth at the teacher, snapping at him, its eyes glaring venomously. But with some fear in them, Harris noticed, almost with satisfaction. What's happened to its inscrutability now? It's scared. Of me! He cried out in blood-lust, bringing the poker down hard upon the thin skull. It split wide open and substance flowed out, the whole body stiffening and them going limp.

Harris felt sick. Killing even monstrosities like this held no pleasure, no triumph. He backed away, knowing the body now blocking the exit for the other rats wouldn't last long. It would either be pushed through or its hind-quarters eaten away.

Even as he walked backwards, he saw the body jerking, as though being tugged from behind. Suddenly, half its body dropped from the hole. That's all it took, he thought. Less than half-a-minute to chew away its hind-quarters! Another black shape began to push its way through. Harris turned and ran, first throwing the poker back at the door, more in frustration than in panic. It missed the rat and clattered to the floor.

The rat was through, another taking its place immediately as it dashed towards the retreating teacher.

The door opened slowly because of the pressure from the few inches of water at its base and Harris barely made it in time. As he slipped through and pulled it shut behind him, he heard the heavy thud of the rat's body crashing into the other side. Clawing noises soon followed. There was nothing on the stairs that he could jam against the door. He raced up the stairs and through to the next floor, slamming the door shut behind him. He burst into the Headmaster's study, giving Ainsley a fright. The Headmaster still seemed to be in a state of shock.

Harris ran to the window and leaned out. Ladders from the fire-engines had already been extended to the adjacent classroom windows and firemen were about to clamber in.

"Over here!" he cried. "Bring one over here – with a hose."

One of the firemen looked across at him. "The hoses are being used below sir," he said, then added, "Don't worry. We'll get to you in a moment, sir. Soon as we've seen to the children."

"Get a hose up here quickly!" he shouted impatiently. "We've got to stop the bloody things getting up the stairs!"

Without further argument, the firemen began to descend.

"Mr. Harris, there is no need for one to lose one's temper." Grimble's head was sticking out from a nearby classroom window. "If we all remain calm . . ."

"Shit!"

Grimble's head disappeared abruptly. Harris smiled to himself. At least he was getting *some* satisfaction from today. He looked down to see the firemen talking to his superiors, pointing out his window. He saw them nod and the firemen run over to where two others were controlling a hose. The streaming jet of water died and the heavy hose was manhandled towards the base of the long ladder. The first fireman mounted the steps carrying the metal hose point over his shoulder, his colleagues paying it out as he ascended.

Harris noticed a white van bearing the name of "Ratkill" had arrived. Men in white overalls were unloading several long silver cylinders. He assumed it was some sort of gas. The whole street was blocked now by police cars, fire engines, ambulances, and the crowds were being held back by a cordon of policemen at both ends. He saw anxious parents, the women crying, pleading with the police to be let through.

As the fireman neared the top of the ladder, it was swung over towards Harris's window.

"Good," he said, helping the man into the room.

"Which way is it?" the fireman asked looking round, ignoring Ainsley and the Headmaster.

"Straight through. Follow me," said Harris, pulling more of the hose through the window. He noted more uniformed figures were climbing up.

They both carried the hose through into the corridor.

"Just a minute," said the teacher, halting in front of the door to the stairs. "Let's just check first." He wondered if he would ever be able to open a door confidently again as he peeped through the merest crack. He opened it wide when he saw it was safe. They went down to the bend in the stairs and looked at the closed door below. The fireman looked at Harris as he heard the clawing noise coming from it.

"My Gawd, is that them?" he asked.

"Yes," said Harris. "It's them. Gnawing their way through. It won't take them long either – they've got teeth like electric saws."

"Well, the place seems to be filling up with water all right," said the fireman, removing his helmet and scratching his head.

Harris nodded. There were three or four inches of water at least at the foot of the stairs. "The basement must be completely flooded by now. Up to the windows anyway, and the jet from the hoses must be preventing any rats from getting out."

They heard footsteps behind them. Three policemen, one a sergeant and two more firemen were coming down to join them.

Harris gestured to them to stay where they were. "The rats are trying to break through the door. If one of your men stands at the window, another by the study door and another at the top of the stairs, we can signal back for the right moment for the water to be turned on."

"The only trouble is, we'll only be able to use half-power,

because of the bends," said the fireman at his side. "If we use full power, the force will try to straighten the hose out."

"Let's try and make all the curves fairly rounded then," said the sergeant. "No sharp turns."

They formed the hose in a series of curving arcs around the various corners.

"The force will throw it against the right hand wall, so I'll stand there and hold it off. Harry, you get on the other side," said the fireman at the teacher's side.

The sergeant ordered the other fireman back to the window upstairs, and his two men into strategic positions along the way.

"Right. Let the bleeders come," he said.

They waited in silence, watching tiny cracks grow larger in the door below.

"Get ready up there!" the first fireman bellowed. "It's unbelievable. Solid wood."

"Yes, and this is the second time this morning," commented the burly sergeant.

"What do you mean?" Harris asked.

"They attacked a train-load of people in the rush-hour. We don't know the strength of it yet, but it seems it was a massacre. Didn't believe it, myself, 'til I saw this lot."

"A train-load of people? They attacked a train?" Harris stared incredulously at the policeman. "I don't believe it."

"Oh, it's true enough," replied the sergeant. "As I said, we don't know all the facts yet. It could have been exaggerated. But we were called out last night as well, to Shadwell. Three people dead. We found what was left of the Station-master – which wasn't much – inside a cupboard. The door had been cracked open. They were going to try and hush it up for a while, but you can't keep something like *this* quiet."

They heard the splinter of wood and a hole appeared in the door, spreading upwards as a large chunk was dislodged.

"Right!" shouted the fireman.

"Right, right, right" came the echoes from the other men.

A rat began to wriggle through the hole.

The lifeless hose stiffened as it filled with water and the fireman released the jet immediately, aiming it directly at the squirming creature. It hit the door a fraction of a second too late. The rat scrambled free just in time, its hind-quarters being knocked aside by the powerful liquid jet. The fireman aimed low, throwing it back against the wall.

"The door. Concentrate on the door. Don't let any more get through," shouted Harris, but it was already too late. With lightning speed, another rat had leapt through the exposed hole. The fireman returned his jet to the door, completely covering the hole, and in fact, making it bigger by pushing the loose pieces inwards. The two free rats half-ran, half-swam towards the stairs.

"I'll deal with them," roared the sergeant, snatching one of the firemen's small axes from his belt. He advanced towards the approaching rats taking care to keep out of the path of the cascading water. To gain him more time, the fireman lowered his aim for a split second, sending the two creatures sprawling back against the opposite wall.

The policeman jumped the last two steps and landed with a splash, brandishing the axe above his head. He slipped, but lashed out at one of them as he did, managing to cut deep into its back. Once again, the child-like squeal of the injured monster. Without waiting to do further damage, he turned on the second rat, but only hitting it a glancing blow with the flat of the axe. It fell back, twisted round, and launched itself at the big man's legs. The policeman cried out as the vicious teeth sank into his knee. He hit sideways at the tenacious beast, wary of cutting his own leg with his bloodied weapon, trying to dislodge it. In desperation, he fell to one knee, pushed the rat flat against the ground, and brought the axe down with all his might. He almost cut the black-furred body in half.

The other injured rat tried to make it to the stairs but Harris ran forward and kicked it back as it mounted the first step. The policeman chopped its head off with one stroke. Then he prised the jaws of the rat still clinging to his knee loose. He limped up the side of the steps, cursing loudly.

The fireman who had been stationed at the window came running down. "They've just brought the cylinders of gas into the playground. They're going to feed it into the windows. They said it's harmless to humans providing you don't get too much of it, but lethal to vermin – cover your faces with wet handkerchiefs to stop yourselves choking on it."

"Tell them to pour gas into the window around the side of the building. It's the staff-room window – they may try to get back out that way!" Harris shouted above the noise of gushing water.

"Right!" The fireman raced back up the stairs.

"Think you can hold them?" Harris asked the man with the hose.

"No problem. Even if the door bursts open under the pressure, we can keep them off the stairs until the gas gets them!"

Harris helped the sergeant with his torn knee up to the second floor. As he limped along, the policeman said: "I've been told these bites can be dangerous. Didn't the kid who died from one last week come from this school?"

"Yes, he did. His name was Keogh."

"That's right. He must have been pretty badly bitten, wasn't he?"

"I don't know," Harris lied.

He took him into the Headmaster's study and sat him on a straight-backed chair.

"Oh dear. Have you been wounded too?" Ainsley asked querulously, reaching for the medicine box.

"Only the one bite, sir. Nothing much. Just stings a bit," the policeman told him.

Harris went along to the next-door classroom and rapped on the door.

"It's all right," he called out. "Let me in."

He heard the grating of furniture being dragged back and the door was opened to him. The room was completely full now with teachers, pupils, policemen and firemen.

He raised his hand for the children to be quiet. "Everything's under control now. The stairs are being blocked by water, and gas – harmless to us – is being pumped into the classrooms downstairs. We should be able to leave fairly soon."

"Thank you very much for your appraisal of the situation, Mr. Harris", Grimble said acidly. "I'm sure the Chief-

Inspector can take charge now. With your permission, of course."

There's one rat the gas won't destroy, Harris thought.

The rats in the school were slowly exterminated. The ones not drowned in the basement were finished off by the gas. The others on the ground-floor scurried around, swimming through the rising water, frantically looking for a means of escape. They climbed on top of radiators, gnawed through doors into classrooms and tried to escape through the windows only to be stopped by the meshwork grill fixed to the outside frames. They jumped onto desk-tops, cupboards, anything above ground level, to escape the torrent of water. Then gas seeped through and one by one, convulsing violently, rearing up on their hind legs, they finally dropped, some into the water, others sprawling on the tops that might have saved them from drowning.

Many tried again and again to crawl through the hole in the door at the end of the corridor, but were beaten back by the powerful jet of water. Their panic caused a madness in them. They fought amongst themselves, whenever they collided or whenever more than one tried to reach the same point of safety. Then a pack would single out one particular rat for no apparent reason, and attack it, killing it in a matter of seconds because no resistance was offered. Then the pack would pick on one of its own members and destroy it. Thus the numbers were depleted.

Soon, they were all dead.

Chapter 12

It became known as "Black Monday" for Londoners. Reports came in at regular intervals all day long; reports of deaths and injuries. The Underground tragedy was the major disaster, the school had almost been the second. Deaths occurred in bizarre ways: the man who went to get his car out and found his garage full of the vermin; the baby left in his pram in the morning sun, laughing at the black creatures, to be dragged out and killed; the priest saying his morning devotions, alone in his church; the two electricians rewiring an old house for new tenants; a pensioner, living in the top of a new council building, opening her front door to take in her milk; the dustman who took off a dustbin lid to find two creatures lurking inside.

There were miraculous escapes too; a postman delivering letters to a basement flat turned to find three sets of evil-looking eyes staring at him from a coal bunker – the rats made no attempt to attack him as he stumbled backwards up the stone steps; a gang of dockers were trapped by rats in a dockside shed – they escaped by climbing stacked crates, through the skylight and across the roof; a milkman warded off two black rats by throwing milk bottles at them; a housewife found her hall filled with the creatures – she ran upstairs and jumped from a bedroom window into the street.

But perhaps the most fantastic escape of all was the newspaper boy, on his early-morning round, who took a short cut across debris to find himself in the midst of thirty or forty giant rats. Amazingly cool for a fourteen-year-old boy, he calmly walked through them, taking great care not to tread on any. For no apparent reason, they let him pass without harm. The boy would never have been believed save for the fact he was seen from the road by two men on their way to work. There was no explanation for the phenomenon, no logical reason.

People in Stepney, where most of the incidents occurred, were in a state of fear – and anger. They blamed the local authorities for the whole situation, insisting that proper sanitation for the area had never been maintained to its full and proper extent. Old bomb-sites had been neglected since the war; houses that were condemned for years still remained standing; garbage from markets and rubbish dumps were never cleared soon enough. All breeding places for filth – all sanctuaries for vermin. The local councils blamed the government, implying that the investigation carried out by the Department of Health was not thorough; that not enough money had been allotted to the task of destroying the pests; that too little time and labour had been allowed on the project; that not enough care had been taken to ensure the total extinction of the vermin. The government ordered a public inquiry in which the ultimate responsibility was laid squarely and irrevocably on the shoulders of Foskins, the Under-Secretary of State.

He accepted responsibility and resigned, knowing it was expected of him. The Ratkill organisation came in for stiff criticism too. They were accused of negligence and publicly reprimanded by the government but claimed they were dealing with an unknown and unpredictable species of rodent. They asked to be given another chance to tackle the menacing problem and were informed that virtually every pest-control organisation in the country was in fact to be brought in to deal with the situation, and all were to work strictly in conjunction with one another.

It became a political issue, the Labour Party claiming the Conservatives, the party in power, never *really* cared about the living conditions of the working-class people and had neglected to clear slums, allowed filth to pile up in the streets and had never implemented proposed plans (proposed by Labour when they were in office) for a completely new network of sewers to cope with London's vast waste problem. The Conservatives replied that the living conditions of London's working class had not suddenly degenerated when their party had taken over Parliamentary power, but had been allowed to deteriorate by the previous Labour government. They quoted statistics of huge new development areas, not just in London's East End, but in every poorer section of the city. Pollution, they said, was being rescinded dramatically.

All eastern regions of the city's Underground were temporarily shut down until a full purge of all tunnels had been completed. However, most people declined to use any section of the Tube system and rush hours became chaotic. Dockers came out on strike, refusing to work in dockside areas where the menace seemed strongest. Dustmen refused to risk their lives clearing rubbish that could contain the deadly vermin. Troops were called in to deal with the problem – rubbish could not be allowed to accumulate at such a precarious time. The municipal workers who maintained the sewers naturally resisted any persuasion to continue their work.

When news of the deaths from the disease carried by the rats became known, matters became even more critical.

People living in the East London boroughs demanded immediate evacuation. The government urged them to remain calm – the situation was firmly under control. Parents refused to send their children to school. The war-time measure of child evacuation came into being once more and the children were shunted off to all parts of the country. Poisons were laid in cellars, gardens and dustbins, killing small rats, mice and many household pets. Restaurants were mistrusted and not used. Many butchers decided to close up shop for a while – the thought of being amongst all that raw meat proved to be too uncomfortable. Any job that entailed working beneath

ground was turned down. Any job that involved night-work
was refused.

The attacks continued and more people died from injuries
or disease, or both.

Although the pest control companies were meant to be
working together on counter measures against the apparent
rat invasion, each tried to out-do the other in finding the solu-
tion. Poisons proved fairly ineffectual for the rats seemed to
feed mainly on human or animal flesh. Sodium Fluoroacetate
and Fluoracetamide were used after the normal poisons, Zinc
Phosphide and Arsenious Oxide, had failed, but these too
seemed to have little effect.

Gas, as had been proved in the attack on the school, was
the effective answer, but the rats had to be caught in a confined space. It was poured into sewers and basements of old
buildings but when teams of men wearing protective clothing
were sent down to investigate the results, they found many
dead normal-sized rats but only a small number of dead giant
rats.

Harris was staring out of the window of his flat when the
phone rang. He'd been gazing at the small private park set in
the square, surrounded by tall, terraced houses, magnificent
in their Regency days but slightly dilapidated now. The teacher was waiting to be assigned to another school now that St.
Michael's and others in that area had been shut down until
matters were improved. His mind always became more relaxed
when he studied the peaceful little park, and after the ordeal
in the school, his taut nerves needed all the relaxation they
could get.

He answered the 'phone, its shrill cry stirring up the tension
again.

"Hello, Mr. Harris? Foskins here."

After this initial surprise, Harris answered. "Hello, Foskins
What can I. . . .?"

"We wondered if you could help us in a small way, old
chap?"

"Well, of course, I . . ."

"Just a few questions some of our boys would like to ask

you. Nothing much, shouldn't take long. You see, it turns out that you're one of the very few people that have had actual contact with these killer rats and lived. If you could come along this afternoon . . .?"

"Right. But I thought you'd been. . . ."

"Dismissed? On the surface, I have, old boy, had to be. Public demand. But I'm afraid the Ministry rather needs me at this particular time, so don't believe everything you read in the papers. Now, here's the address I want you to come to. . . ."

He was greeted by Foskins himself when he arrived at the address he'd been given. It had turned out to be Poplar Town Hall, a natural enough base for operations, he supposed. Foskins led him to a large assembly room, the walls covered with enlarged maps of the area, diagrams of the Underground and sewage networks, blow-ups of the giant rats themselves vivisected as well as whole, even photographs of their spoors.

The room was a hive of activity but Foskins took him over to a group of men gathered round a table in quiet, unexcited discussion.

"Gentlemen, this is Mr. Harris, the teacher I told you of," Foskins introduced him. "This is our team of experts. Researchers from the major pest-control companies, biologists, sanitation experts from our own department – even a couple of chemical warfare chaps!"

He nodded hello.

"Let me just briefly bring you up to date and then we'll put some questions to you," said Foskins. "We've examined these monsters thoroughly and haven't really found anything unusual about them apart from their size of course, and their slightly larger brain. Their teeth are bigger, but only in proportion to their body. Their ears, which seem peculiarly long at first because of their nakedness, are also in exact proportion to their body. But the Black rats normally have longer ears than the brown species. Which brings us to an interesting point." He paused, indicating that Harris should take a seat, then went on: "The Brown Rat seems to have vanished from London. Since the Brown rat is unable to climb as well as the Black, over the years it has had less chance to survive in the

city. Whereas the Black rat is able to scale walls and leap
across rooftops, the Brown has found it increasingly harder
to gain access into premises that have barriers against them.
For years, the two species have been battling for superiority
and now it appears that the Black have won. We've found no
trace of the Brown, not even its spoors which are quite different from those of the Black."

"It's natural to assume that the introduction of the freak
giant Black rats tipped the balance," interrupted one of the
group of men.

"Yes, rather like a small country acquiring the Hydrogen
bomb, continued Foskins. "Well, it seems they completely
vanquished the Brown rat. One of our younger members,"
he looked at the man who had just spoken, "came up with
the idea of bringing back multitudes of the Brown to do battle
with the Black, giving them the advantage of numbers. Need-
less to say, we have no intention of turning East London into
a battleground for vermin. The consequences could have been
disastrous."

The young researcher turned a deep red and studied his
finger-nails intently.

"So this is the villain we face." Foskins held up a photograph of a large, but dead, rat. *Rattus rattus.* Black rat. Or
Ship rat. There are some of the species known to be this size
in tropical countries. We think a member, or members of that
species came over in a ship and bred with our own common
variety. Because of the difficulties involved, we suspect they
were brought over secretly. The zoos claim no knowledge of
such an undertaking and as the whole idea would be illegal anyway, we don't expect an individual to come forward to admit
it."

"Now what we want from you, Mr. Harris, is information,"
said another member of the committee. "Anything at all that
might tell us more about these creatures. You see, we haven't
managed to capture any alive yet and you are the one person
that has had close contact with them on more than one occa-
sion and lived. We don't know anything of their behaviour
pattern, where they go after they've attacked, why sometimes
they won't attack at all, and what's caused their hunger for

human flesh. The slightest peculiarity you may have noticed could be of invaluable help to us."

Harris told them of his experiences with the rats; about Keogh, one of their first victims, and how they had chased the boy along the canal, scaling a six-foot wall but letting him escape; the episode with Ferris, the little man from Ratkill, and of their first sighting of the vermin, swimming in a kind of formation; how one had stopped on the opposite bank of the canal to study him, suddenly disappearing through the fence.

"Did you frighten it, is that what made it go?" he was asked.

"No, No. It wasn't fear. It seemed to raise its head, as though it had suddenly heard something, almost as if it had been called. But I heard nothing."

One of the researchers spoke up. "They do have an acute sense of hearing, as do many animals or mammals. Rats can locate their offspring in a field of corn by its high-pitched whistle. Nothing unusual. In fact, my company is working on a method of rooting out rats from buildings by the use of ultrasonic sound beams. It's in its early stages as yet, but it certainly seems to work."

"Well, maybe that was it. But it *is* unusual the way they study you. It's happened more than once, almost as if they're reading your mind. It's uncanny." He went on to tell them of the battle in the school, relating every detail he could remember. When he'd concluded there was silence around the table.

"Sorry, it's not much help to you," he said, feeling he'd left something out, his mind groping unclearly towards it.

"On the contrary, Mr. Harris," smiled Foskins, "it's been quite useful. Now if you leave us to digest the information you've given us. . . ."

The young researcher whom Foskins had caused to blush earlier sprang to his feet excitedly. "Infect them" he cried.

All eyes turned towards him.

"Look, we can't poison them because they only want human or animal flesh. But we could infect them."

"How exactly?" asked the sceptical Foskins.

"We inject a group of animals – dogs, cats – what about Brown rats? – with a virus, something highly infectious, deadly to rats – our bio-chemists could easily come up with one – set them loose at certain points that Mr. Harris could show us – that section of the canal, for instance – the infected animals are attacked by the Black rats, they themselves are infected, they spread it amongst their own kind. They destroy themselves!"

There was silence for a few moments.

"It could infect people. It could cause an epidemic," someone ventured.

"Not if we used the right virus."

"It could kill all the animals in and around London."

"It's worth the risk, isn't it?"

More silence.

Then Foskins said: "You know, it might just work."

The young researcher beamed a smile of gratitude.

"Yes, it might," one of the scientists leaned forward enthusiastically. "They're too bloody clever to be baited with poison – or they're immune to it. But if we could infect them . . ."

"Not with rats though," said another, the idea, perhaps out of desperation, begining to catch fire. "Too much of a risk with other rats. Too unpredictable."

"All right, dogs then. Pups, to make it easier for the rats."

Harris's mind rebelled at the idea of feeding young pups to vermin.

"Why not just infect raw meat?" he suggested.

"No, the virus would have to exist on living flesh."

"But how do we know what virus? We haven't got a live giant rat in captivity. How do we know which virus would kill it?" asked Foskins.

"I have a pretty good idea already," said a bio-chemist. "We can test it on the normal Black rat – and hope it will work on its larger brother."

The debate continued, arguments flared, solutions found. Harris felt quite flattered to be involved in the centre of the operation, but his mind still nagged him about something forgotten.

"Very well," Foskins finally drew the discussion to its noisy conclusion." It shouldn't take more than a few days to find the right virus. Although it must be tested thoroughly – I needn't stress how thoroughly – we should be ready to put the plan into action by the middle of next week. In the meantime, Mr. Harris and I, together with the Borough surveyor will work to find the most suitable locations for deploying the infected dogs. Mr. Harris was brought up in this area, I might add, so I presume knows most of the likely places the rats might use as lairs. You will all carry on with your usual activities of laying poisons, using gas or anything else you may think of, and we'll assemble every morning at eight-thirty to see how things are going. Are there any questions? No? Good. Let's get on with it then." He turned to Harris, and said quietly, "Join me for a drink, Mr. Harris."

They crossed the road from the Town Hall and entered a pub just opening its doors for the early evening rush. Their eyes adjusted to the gloom reluctantly after the bright sunshine of late afternoon. "What will you have?" Foskins asked, reaching for his wallet.

"Keg."

"Pint of Keg and a gin and tonic, please."

They found a quiet corner and relaxed into imitation leather seats.

"Cheers," said Foskins.

"Good health," replied Harris.

They drank in silence for a few moments.

"I'm surprised," said Harris.

"At what?"

"That you're still running things."

"Ah, that. As I explained over the telephone, Mr. Harris, the public wanted somebody's head, I was in charge, I was the only choice." He smiled thinly, his eyes examining the rim of his glass. "A scapegoat always has to be found – it's the way things are." He quickly shrugged off his dejected mood, and smiled at the teacher. "But I'm too good at m'job for them to do without me and they – the indefinable they – are well aware of it. You see, the only mistake I made last time was in underestimating the foe. A bad mistake, I grant you. It certainly had serious consequences. But under the circumstances, it was a natural error, don't you agree? I mean, it's not the sort of thing that happens every day, is it?"

"I suppose not." Harris took a long drink, feeling Foskins eyes on him.

"You were rather harsh on me yourself, last time we met," Foskins said.

It suddenly dawned on Harris why he had become involved in the operation. He wasn't really that necessary – *he'd* hardly call his help invaluable. Foskins had been mistreated by the public. Mistreated and unappreciated. They'd yelled for his blood and his superiors had given it to them. On the surface, anyway. And he himself had scorned him. So Harris, in a symbolic way, represented the public. He was Foskins' actual contact with the people who had derided him. And now he was going to prove them wrong. Through him. Showing he was still in command, and very, very able.

Good *luck*! thought Harris.

"Well, it seems we've had quite a breakthrough today." Foskins setted back in his seat, a broad smile on his face. "Don't know why we didn't think of it before. Like another drink?"

"Let me," said Harris, draining his glass and rising to his feet. "Same again?"

He brought the drinks back to the table, catching the other man deep in thought. Foskins looked up at him, almost as though he were a stranger.

"Thank you," he said. "Well, I think we've cracked it now, don't you? Yes, things will soon be back to normal. You'll be back at your school, I'll be re-instated – not publicly, of course, or perhaps moved to another department. Not dishonourably though." He sipped his gin. "Tell me, what makes you teach in the East End? There are more pleasant places aren't there?"

"Home ground."

"Oh, so you live here still?"

"No, I've got a flat near Kings Cross."

"Married? Must be."

"No, not really."

"I see. I used to be."

Foskins took a large gulp from his drink, his mind drifting

away again. Harris began to get slightly irritated by the melancholy turn the conversation kept taking.

"Do you think they'll come up with the right virus in time?" he asked, changing the subject.

"Oh, yes. No problem. Those boys could come up with a way to make fleas catch German Measles. Time is the important factor. Do you know how fast these bloody rats breed. Five to eight times a year. And their offspring can breed within three months. You're a teacher, you work it out; if we don't kill the bloody things soon, they'll over-run the whole city. Have another drink?"

"No, I've got to go," said Harris. "Someone waiting."

"Yes, yes, of course." Dejected once again. "Well, see you bright and early tomorrow then, eh?" More brightly.

"You want me to come along then?"

"Why, yes. You're involved now, old chap. Don't worry about your people. I'll clear it with them. As a matter of fact, I already have. Sure you won't have another. Right. I'll see you tomorrow."

Harris left the pub with relief. He wasn't quite sure why he disliked Foskins — perhaps it was his unpredictable moods. One minute bright, hearty, efficient, the next — well, "hangdog" was the only expression that sprang readily to mind. Harris couldn't wait to get home to Judy.

Foskins stared moodily into his glass. Mustn't stay here too long, I suppose, he thought to himself. Wouldn't do to have any of his staff pop in from across the road and catch him drinking by himself. Wouldn't look good, expecially just now.

He wondered about the young teacher. Probably living with a girl — didn't look queer. Sure of himself, self-contained. Young. Might be useful in this exercise, though. Not essential of course, but at least the teacher would learn just how difficult it was to organize a project like this. The experience would do him a lot of good — only wish *more* people had some idea of the difficulties involved, then perhaps they wouldn't be so ready to cry for blood at the first crisis. They'll soon see I'm not ready for the shelf just yet.

He ordered another drink — just a quick one, he told himself — and returned to his seat.

Funny how things turn out, he brooded. Always having to prove yourself to others. To some it comes easy, they're born with the gift, but for the others it requires constant, hard work, not relaxing for a minute, never revealing your weakness to those who'd be only too pleased to turn it to their own advantage. That's how it's always been for me. Work, leadership – they've never come easily. Always the struggle a well-guarded secret. If only they knew of the night hours spent in sheer slog, sheer tedious grind, to keep up with the work output. Not just keep up, but to be ahead of.

But Rosemary had found out. She had to of course – she was my wife. Any other woman would have offered consolation, but not Rosemary. She grew bored with the nights spent plodding through paperwork. And when she discovered that prowess in bed was also a task that didn't come naturally to me – well, the disillusionment was too great. If we'd had children I suppose she'd have had something to occupy her, but she even blamed me for that. Nevertheless, it lasted for fifteen years so she must have felt some love for me. Even though, I knew she was having the odd affair, it didn't really matter as long as she was discreet. Even her jibes in front of friends, and colleagues, I could have survived by ridiculing her in return in that false-hearty way. But when her affairs became much more frequent and much less discreet – and worst of all, much less discriminating, then it had to be brought to an end. But she jumped the gun by ending it first, walking out, running off with a bloody travel agent! A travel agent! Did my best to hush things up, but word always gets around, so there was nothing left but to work even harder, to become more successful, anything to cover the shame of being left high and dry by an unfaithful wife. And the double-shame of having been cuckolded by her and a damn travel agent! How could you retain your dignity after that? But I managed it, worked myself up into this position. Yes, there was the affair of the rats that had done some damage to my esteem, but my superiors wouldn't let me go, would they? No they know my true worth. Public be damned. And when this little episode is over, they'll all acknowledge my worth. The fact of the matter is, the more power you have, the easier it is to find solutions to any problems. You merely surround yourself with the right people, the right brains – they come up with the answers and you take the glory. The hard part was to gain that position of authority, but once you had it, the rest was easy.

I'll just have one more drink and then perhaps I'll go along to the club, tell the boys all is going well, drop a few hints about our idea, not too much, in case it doesn't work, but enough to let them know old Foskins has done it again. Feel better now, no point in going home to an empty house just yet. The boys'll be pleased to see me, I should think.

He drained his glass and walked out into the still bright sunshine.

Harris reported at eight-thirty every morning to the daily Town Hall meetings. He worked out with Foskins and the Borough surveyors ten key locations that they considered to be likely rat-infested spots. By the end of the week, the biochemists had come up with the correct virus.

They laughed at the teacher's admiration for their speed. "That wasn't the problem," they told him. "You see, we've had the virus itself for many years. In fact, we inherited it from the Germans after the war. They'd been working on a way of killing off all our livestock by infection without harming the population and they had actually come up with the answer. Fortunately, for us, the war ended before they had time to use it and it's been a well-kept secret, along with a few other nasty little items, ever since. The hard part – and this has taken the time – was to find an antidote to contain it. We don't relish the idea of wiping out all animal life in the country. Well, we've found the antitoxin and it will be a simple matter to introduce it into our animals, either by injection or mixing it with their food or water. It's already being produced in bulk, and, just as a safeguard, we're working on another serum in case the first fails. As a safeguard, we must stress. We see absolutely no reason for the first to let us down."

Foskins congratulated them on their fine work and they set a time to put the plan into action.

"Very well, gentlemen," concluded the minister. "On Tuesday morning, at six, we'll plant the first infected puppies.

We'll go on to nine other locations throughout the morning, all key points, and leave the unfortunate but expendable animals to their fate. Any questions?"

"Yes," said Harris, raising his hand but quickly dropping it realizing he was emulating his absent pupils. "What happens, when we're planting the pups, if we become the victims of the rats?"

"Everyone is to wear protective clothing, Mr. Harris. It's standard procedure on any operation like this. I think you'll find the suits adequate even if uncomfortable." Foskins looked around at the faces. "Any more questions?"

"Yes," said Harris.

"Mr. Harris?"

"What if it doesn't work."

"If what doesn't work?"

"The idea."

"Then God help us, Mr. Harris."

The grey dawn cast a mist over the old canal. Not even a bird disturbed the chill morning silence. The dirty waters stirred occasionally in the slight dawn breeze, sending small ripples lapping lazily at the stone sides of the man-made river.

The silence was broken by a tiny yelp. Along the bank came five men looking like visitors from another planet. They were covered from head to foot in a heavy, plastic-like material and wearing helmets with large glass visors. Two of the men carried a large basket. The lid bounced now and again as if the occupants of the container were striving to get free. One of the men motioned towards a spot by the side of the canal and the basket was placed on the ground.

"This should do for the first lot," said Harris, sweating inside his heavy suit. He lifted the glass visor so the others could hear him more clearly.

"This is where we saw the rats last time. They were swimming along the canal up to this point. Then they climbed out and disappeared through that hole over there." He pointed towards the other bank.

The basket was opened and three small dogs were lifted out. Harris fondled one of them affectionately. Poor little bleeder, he thought.

The young researcher, introduced to the teacher after their first meeting at the Town Hall as Stephen Howard, lifted his visor and wiped his brow with a gloved hand. "Well, let's chain two down and let the other wander," he said. "That way, the rats are bound to get them."

Harris watched as a metal stake was driven into the hard path that ran alongside the muddy canal and two of the pups were chained to it.

"All right, little'n, off you go." He placed the pup he was holding on the ground and gave it a gentle shove, but it pushed back against his hand, licking it and looking up at him.

"Go on, boy, it's for Queen and country."

The pup squatted on its haunches and looked up at him. "Oh Christ;" muttered Harris, "it's going to be more difficult than I thought."

Howard reached into the basket and brought out some raw meat. "This should tempt him. It's meant as rat bait, but I don't see why these little blighters shouldn't enjoy a last meal. I'll entice him along to the bridge and leave him there with enough to feast on. Here boy, come on." He bumped the meat against the pup's nose and trailed it along tantalizingly just above it's snapping jaws.

"Don't go too far!" shouted Harris, as the strangely-clad figure disappeared underneath the bridge. He and the others began to scatter more raw meat around the two remaining puppies, feeding them a little to keep them happy.

They looked up at the sound of running feet to see Howard coming towards them, waving his arms excitedly. At first, they couldn't understand his shouts, but as he pointed back towards the bridge they realized why he was making such haste to get away from it.

In the gloom under the bridge they saw several black-shaped creatures surrounding the pup, which had begun to whine piteously. Harris made as if to move towards it, but a restraining hand was placed on his arm. He nodded, seeing the sense of it. What did it matter if a pup lost its life when countless people were to be saved because of it? But it was a horrible way for the poor little mite to go.

Suddenly they saw a line of rats break out from the dark interior of the bridge and streak out after the lumbering researcher. The leading rat swiftly caught up with the suit-clumsy figure and leapt at the plodding legs. It clung to the material of the suit but its razor-sharp teeth failed to penetrate. Howard continued to run, dragging the persistent creature along with him.

"Your visor," shouted Harris. "Close your visor!"

Howard heard him and snapped the glass protection shut. He stumbled as another rat attached itself to his other leg, but managed to keep on his feet. The group of men looked on in horror as another scaled his back and perched on his shoulder, snapping at his head covering. He went down heavily, one arm splashing into the canal water. He raised himself to his knees, rats swarming all over him now. He tried in vain to brush them off, but they clung to his body like giant leeches.

Harris saw what he feared most – a tear beginning to appear in the tough material. He ran forward, the three other men following. Reaching Howard, he began pulling at the rats which were now tearing at the cloth in frenzy, oblivious to the blows being dealt them. Harris kicked two into the canal, hoping they were stunned enough to drown, and ignoring the clinging creatures, he dragged the researcher to his feet and pulled him along the canal bank.

All the men were fighting for their own lives now as more of the rodents poured over them. They staggered on, back towards the gap in the fence that would allow them to escape from the death-trap canal. Some of the pressure was taken off them as they passed the two howling pups and the littered raw meat, for the rats pounced on the easier prey with relish.

"Back to the vans!" Harris heard a muffled shout. "We've got the gas cylinders there!"

They kept going, the way easier now for most of the rats were converging on the animal flesh. Helping one another, they reached the gap and climbed through. Abruptly, the rats still clinging dropped to the ground as if they sensed the danger to themselves once outside the boundary to the canal. Harris lunged at one before it could escape, ignoring the revulsion within him caused by the squirming creature. He held onto its neck with one hand its back legs with the other and' lifted it high into the air.

"Here's a live specimen for you!" he cried, struggling to keep his grasp.

"Good man," shouted Howard and dashed forward to help the teacher. The giant rat was immensely strong and struggled fiercely in their arms, but the two men held on grimly. The other rats, which had not fled, but had remained on the other side of the gap, suddenly came through and began to attack the two men.

The other three kicked and pulled at the vermin, trying to beat them off but it soon became apparent that their efforts would be wasted unless they had more help. Their companions in the nearby vans started their engines and roared towards them, screeching to a halt by the side of the melée. The back doors of the walk-through vans were flung open and the struggling men began to clamber in, the rats clinging to them and leaping into the two vehicles. The noise was deafening to Harris, even through the protection of the helmet; the pups in their baskets barking furiously, the vermin squealing in their peculiar high-pitched fashion, the shouts and cries of the men. He realised the driver of the van he'd made for wasn't wearing his helmet or gloves. He shouted at the man to cover his head and hands but the driver failed to hear above the clamour. Two men were inside the first van now and were swiftly unpacking the gas tanks, kicking at the rats as they leapt into the interior. Harris and Howard climbed in holding their captive between them, ignoring the pain of bites that did not penetrate, but squeezed their flesh in excruciating pinches. The van began to move forward, the rats chasing it and trying to leap through the open back doors, some making it, others being kicked back onto the road. The doors were slammed shut, jamming in the middle on the body of a rat which fell out again with the help of a sharp kick from one of the men.

The gas in one of the cylinders was released to deal with the vermin left inside the van and still persisting in their attack.

"Not this one!" ordered Howard. "Find something to put it in. We want it alive!"

A metal box of tools had its contents emptied and the frenzied rat was placed roughly inside. The lid clicked firmly shut. The van's sudden swerving caused them to look anxiously at the driver. He was trying to shake off one of the black beasts from his exposed hand. A jet of gas was aimed at the rat and soon it flopped to the floor at the feet of the driver, whose arm now hung limply at his side. He kept driving, moaning with the pain, but steering with his right hand only. The gas was aimed around the large interior of the vehicle, dealing death within seconds to the vicious rats.

"Not too much gas!" shouted Howard. "We don't want to kill off the dogs as well!"

As the last rat staggered drunkenly then stiffened and died, the men removed their protective helmets and looked towards the injured driver, knowing he was doomed.

"The other van is close behind," said Howard, peering through the back door window. "We're far away enough now," he called to the driver, "so let's pull up and we'll deal with your wound." He looked across at Harris shaking his head in despair.

The van pulled over to the kerbside, the other stopping close behind. The doors were opened and the men wearily climbed out, glad to breathe the fresh morning air after the acrid fumes of the gas. Harris, feeling sick and slightly dizzy, leaned against the side of the van.

"Too much of that gas can kill a man," Howard told him, "especially in a confined space like that. It was lucky we were wearing the helmets. The driver has just blacked out, not from his wound I suspect, but because of the gas – and *he* was near an open window."

"Does the poor sod know he'll die?" asked Harris, his mind still fuzzy.

"Everyone knows about the disease now, Mr. Harris. He was aware of the risk, he should have protected himself."

"Well maybe you haven't been too lucky either," said Harris, pointing at the rip in Howard's suit.

The researcher paled and put his hand to the hole. "I don't

think I've been bitten," he said, "but I'm bruised all over from their teeth. Oh Christ." He fumbled at the zip in the grey suit and managed to pull it down haltingly. To his relief, he found the clothes he wore underneath undamaged. With a deep sigh, he too leaned against the side of the van.

After a while, he said, "Let's take this poor blighter to the hospital, not that it'll do him much good, and then get on with the rounds. Only this time I'm going to get us more protection from Foskin's. I mean, this is only the first location. I hope you've chosen some safe places for us, Harris, in the next nine."

Harris smiled thinly at him. "Are there any safe places around here any more?"

They suffered attacks from the vermin on three other occasions that day. Harris returned to the flat in the evening completely exhausted, both mentally and physically, his nerves almost numbed by the terrors the operation had held. He sank into an armchair and told Judy of the day's events. "The canal was about the worst. It shook us up pretty badly, especially the driver being hurt, so after that we were a bit more cautious. From there we went to the dock area – I've never seen the streets so deserted – left the bait and got out fast." He carefully avoided mentioning the pups, not wanting to upset her, knowing her love of animals.

"But at one spot, we stopped the vans at the entrance of an alley leading to the river, got out and carried the bait to the end of it. We dumped it and turned round to make our way back and found our exit cut off by the bastards. They were streaming from a basement grid. We didn't stop to think – Howard was off like a shot, right through them, and we all followed en masse, kicking and stomping, thanking God for protective suits. We bundled into the vans and got away fast.

"It's funny, but sitting there in the Town Hall, making plans, hearing all the reports, even my own first-hand experiences of the rats – we didn't realize just how bad the situation was. It took today's events to really bring it home. In the morning, the streets were practically deserted, and later on, people were only travelling around in groups or in cars and vans.

"Anyway, after that we met up with our escort promised by Foskins. He'd brought the army into it. Two truckloads of troops armed with water-cannon, flame-throwers, gas – the whole bloody works. It certainly made us feel a bit better."

"You should have started out with them," interrupted Judy, cross not with Harris but at Foskins, who was in control.

"Yes, I know," said Harris, "but we've done it all along. We've underestimated them. Despite all the reports, we've just thought of them as highly dangerous pests, not as the overwhelming force that they seem to be becoming. Even after the train massacre and the attack on the school we didn't expect to meet up with so many of them in one day. True, I'd chosen the most likely places – I had to if our part was to be effective – but even I wasn't prepared for the number of times we came face to face with them. I tell you, Jude, if this doesn't work, that whole area will have to be razed to the ground."

Judy shuddered. "What if it's too late? You told me how fast they breed. What if they spread all over London?"

Harris was silent for a while, then he said: "Goodbye London."

"Oh, darling, let's go now. You've done all you can, you've helped them as much as possible. You said yourself you're not really necessary, you're just there for Foskins' ego. Well let them get on with it. Let's go before it gets worse."

"Come on, Jude, you know we can't. Where would we go"

"Aunt Hazel's for a while. You could be transferred to a local school and I wouldn't mind working in a shop for a while. With all the schools overflowing with evacuated kids they're crying out for more teachers to come out of London."

"No, love. I couldn't leave now. You see, as we drove on today, dressed in those ridiculous space-suits, escorted by soldiers armed to the teeth, and I took them all to places I knew, places familiar to me, places that had been part of my life, I knew I had to see it through. If you like – and I know it may sound silly – it was *my* patch. The men with me were strangers to it. As far as Foskins and his ministry are concerned it could be a foreign land. Oh, I'm not saying I love the area or it's in my blood. Nothing daft like that. But I do feel some responsibility towards it – like it's my old school and it's being demolished by age. See?"

"Yes, I see." Judy smiled at him, holding his hand to her cheek. "You dope."

He shrugged, smiling to himself.

"Any more incidents today?" she asked.

"Yes. In a children's schoolground we saw a score of them attacking a dog, so we drove in and went straight through them, dropping the bait without stopping." Into his mind crowded the terrible sight of his companions dropping the pups from the vans into the midst of the rats, something he'd been unable to take part in. "Later we went into a bombed-out church and discovered the flesh-cleaned bones of two people. Who they were and how long they'd been there we couldn't tell; the skeletons were too clean to have been there too long and there wasn't a trace of clothing. The strange thing was that they were locked in a tight embrace – like lovers. We began to unload the bait when we heard a scream. One of our men had a rat clinging to his neck and was running around like a madman. Fortunately, his suit saved him from serious injury, but his fear was contagious. We all made for the exit. Two men went to the attacked man's aid but soon found they had their own problems. The three of them ran from the opening, rats clinging to their bodies and as soon as they were clear, the water-canon were directed at the gap to stop anything else coming through. The soldiers helped the three men get free of the rats by using their bayonets. The army wanted to fill the place with gas, but Howard wouldn't let them. It was the one time we wanted the rats to live, so they could spread the virus.

"After that episode, we didn't have too much trouble although we still made contact with them. We'd learned to be cautious and kept as close to the vans as possible, leaping inside at the first hint of risk. None of us were very brave, I'm afraid. We were too aware of the consequences."

"I don't want a dead hero, Harris," said Judy.

"Believe me, you won't get one."

"So what happens now?"

"We wait. We wait to see if the virus takes effect and if it does, then it shouldn't take long for it to spread. They reckon within a couple of weeks we'll know one way or another."

"And if it doesn't work, what then?"

"Well it wouldn't just be the East End's problem anymore. They couldn't possibly contain the rats in that area. They'd spread throughout London. And if that happens, I don't want to be around."

Chapter 13

The rats came out onto the streets to die. It was as though having spent their lives scuttling around in the semi-darkness they wished to breathe the fresh air of the upper world before they perished. They littered the streets, their corpses bloated in the sun, at first causing great alarm to the people who lived in the area. The alarm gave way to relief as the people realized the vermin were dying, the crisis was passing. The diseased corpses were gathered up in bulk and loaded into lorries and taken to incinerators where they were reduced to harmless dust. It had taken only two days for the first signs of the virus' effect but it escalated rapidly in the week that followed. There were still attacks on people but they were far less numerous than before. And then a remarkable side-effect of the virus was discovered.

A soldier was bitten by a rat he'd assumed to be dead because of its prone position. He shot it and reported to the hospital where he expected to die. It was extremely critical for three days but he managed to pull through, his survival being attributed to a reaction on the disease carried by the rat from the virus infecting it. The deadly germ had been weakened considerably.

Others bitten by the rats were not quite so fortunate. Some died in the usual twenty-four hours, others lingered on the edge for anything up to a week. Not enough people were bitten to allow any assumptions to be made, but the fact that one person had survived and others had lasted for almost a week was definitely encouraging. Tests were tried on animals but instead of dying from the disease caused by the rats, they died from the man-made virus introduced into the rodents.

After three weeks, the danger from the vermin was thought to be virtually over although only approximately two thousand bodies were found. It was assumed that the rest of the rats' population was dying or dead below ground.

Life began slowly to return to normal. Plans were made to begin a massive clean-up operation on East London's older districts. Houses were to be pulled down, wastelands to either be utilized for building or flattened into concrete playgrounds or car-parks. The dockside areas would be renovated into modern open-plan blocks. Disused basements would be forever sealed, sewers and drains thoroughly cleansed or rebuilt. It would cost millions but a sharp lesson had been learnt. Stepney and Poplar would eventually become fashionable areas and their history of slums forgotten.

Foskins was completely exonerated of any blame for initial mistakes and reinstated publicly to his former position. He was congratulated personally by the Prime Minister and passed on the compliments to the team that had helped him accomplish his critical task. At a press conference he praised the specialists whose painstaking endeavours coupled with their dynamic ingenuity had finally begun to defeat this fearsome mutant creature and the deadly disease it carried, whilst subtly implying all credit really belonged to him, as originator and organizer of the project.

They still held daily meetings in the town hall to discuss the progress of the operation but the urgency was no longer felt amongst the members. A serum was derived from the virus to be used as an antidote for the rat-bites which made the disease non-mortal although now such cases were becoming much less frequent anyway.

The danger had passed. So everyone thought.

Chapter 14

Judy was in the bath, enjoying its cocoon warmth, when she heard the 'phone ring. Harris's muffled voice came through the half-open bathroom door as it was answered. She idly wondered who the caller was. After a few moments of one-sided conversation she heard the click of the receiver being replaced and footsteps crossing the lounge towards the bathroom. Harris came in with a wry smile on his face.

"That was Foskins," he said, sitting on the edge of the toilet.

"Ringing on a Sunday morning? He must miss you."

"Hardly. He's given me the sack."

"What? Why?"

"My services are no longer needed. 'Thank you for your extremely valuable assistance, old boy, but the worst is now over and I think it would be unfair to you to take up any more of your valuable time.'"

"The old bastard."

"No, not really, I couldn't have done any more. To tell you the truth it's a bit of a relief; I've felt a bit useless the last couple of weeks."

"Yes, but to get rid of you now, just when it's nearly all over."

"Well, he's proved his point hasn't he? He doesn't need me to show off to now – he's got the whole of the public. Anyway, the kids will be coming back in a few weeks and then it'll be back to the old routine."

"Hm, I suppose so." Judy settled further down into the water. "But I still think he's an old bastard."

Harris laughed, flickering water gently into her face. "He's invited us to 'a small social gathering' next Tuesday evening."

"What?" Judy sat up again. "I don't believe it!"

"He knows he's a swine and he can't really cope with it. That's probably his weakness – he's only half-bastard." He dipped his hand into the soapy water and trailed his finger along Judy's thigh. "He's doing the dirty on me but he still wants me to love him."

"I see. And do you?"

"It's not really important, is it? I feel sorry for him, in a way, but I don't care one way or the other about our little committee – I'm glad to be out of it. Now the worst is over, I've got better things to do." He stroked the inside of her thigh, her legs parting slightly to allow him access.

"And are we going to his little social gathering?"

"Why not? It'll fill an evening."

Judy murmured in soft appreciation as his hand reached the top of her legs.

"What will you do till the school re-opens?" she asked.

He pulled gently at her small mound of hair, almost pre-occupied with his own thoughts. "I might just have a look round the area; see how things are being cleaned up. Might even do a bit of painting."

"I could get a few days off."

"Aunt Hazel's?"

"Yes, please." She began to squirm in the water and Harris wondered if the "Yes, please" was an affirmation to his question or an encouragement to his exploring fingers.

"Harris," she said.

"Yes?"

"Isn't it time for your bath?"

He began to unbutton his shirt.

Foskins greeted them warmly when they arrived at his home the following Tuesday.

"Hello, old boy, Ah, this must be Judy. Do come in."

Half-plastered already, thought Harris, catching Judy's eye and winking.

"Most of my guests have arrived," said Foskins in an over-loud voice. "Bathroom's upstairs to the left, bedroom to the right."

Judy disappeared up the stairs to attend her make-up and Harris followed Foskins into a room full of chatting people. He saw Howard amongst one of the groups, his face flushed with the glory of the previous week's events. "Hello, Harris!" he called, waving a glass-filled hand and spilling some of its contents on a young woman next to him. "Come and meet everybody."

Harris walked over, Foskins leading him by the arm, taking a Scotch from the waiter with a tray full of assorted drinks on the way. Howard introduced him to his group with an air of camaraderie he'd never shown in their working relationship.

"Oh, you're the teacher who saved all those little children at the school, aren't you?" the girl standing next to Howard said excitedly.

"With the help of half London's police force and fire brigade," smiled Harris.

"Now, my boy, mustn't be modest," said Foskins, placing his hand on the teacher's shoulder and shaking it heartily.

"Fiona adores heroes," Howard laughed, putting a posses-sive arm around her waist.

"Come along, you must meet everybody," Foskins tugged him away from the group. They were joined by Judy as they made their circuit of the room, smiling, shaking hands and being congratulated. After his third Scotch, Harris' mood began to mellow towards the Under-Secretary as he watched him laughing and bantering with his fellow ministers, accepting their praise with mock modesty at one moment and skilful

braggartism the next. He noticed Howard standing to one
side, glaring at Foskins, taking no notice of the chattering
Fiona at his side.

His thoughts were interrupted by Judy whispering in his
ear, "So this is the jet-set?"

"It could have been worse," he smiled down at her. "At
least the booze is flowing smoothly."

"Old Foskins is certainly bathing in the glory."

"Of course. What do you think the party's for? You can't
blame him though."

"Harris, for a belligerent man you're very easy-going."

He laughed, putting an arm around her shoulder and pulling her to him. "All right, he made a mistake once, but he
soon made up for it."

"Yes, with the help of you and all the others!" Judy said
indignantly.

"She's quite right you know, Harris!" Howard had crossed
the room to join them, Fiona at his heels. "He's busy taking
all the credit – very modestly, I grant you – when after all, it
was *my* idea."

"Yes," agreed Fiona, breathlessly.

"And by the way," he added maliciously, "I'm sorry to see
you're no longer part of the team."

Harris grinned at the researcher, refusing to be drawn out.

"What does it matter? It's all over now, anyway," he said,
looking around for the waiter and his tray.

"Yes, and we're all going back eventually to our obscure
little jobs while he . . ."

"Look, if you don't like it, don't tell me about it, tell him."
Harris deftly grabbed a Scotch from the passing tray.

"Right," said Howard. "I bloody will!" and marched to-
ward Foskins.

"Harris, you're evil," Judy admonished the smiling teacher.

"Oh dear, he's going to create a scene," wailed Fiona.

Just as Howard reached the jovial Foskins, the telephone
rang in the hall and the Under-Secretary excused himself from
his group, leaving the researcher standing open-mouthed and
flat-footed.

Harris suppressed his mirth as he watched the researcher gather his wits and stride after him.

Two minutes later, Howard came back into the room ashen-faced. He rejoined them, slowly shaking his head, a look of disbelief on his face.

"Darling, what's the matter, what's happened?" asked Fiona, worriedly.

He looked at each of them in turn, not really seeing their faces. "That 'phone call," he started to say. "It was from our operations room."

They waited in impatient silence.

"There's been another attack. Another massacre – in North London."

Chapter 15

Stephen Abbott sat in the darkened cinema and stole a quick glance at his girlfriend's face, illuminated by the cinemascope screen. He was bored with the film, partly because the big, craggy cowboy on the screen was now too old to act like superman, and partly because he wasn't wearing his glasses. Vikki didn't know he wore glasses sometimes and he thought it might spoil their relationship if she did. She'd probably go off him too if she ever found out about his two false front teeth; he had to be so careful in their "snogging" sessions that her probing tongue didn't dislodge the plate. She was very fussy. And she deserved to be, with her looks! Best looking bird in the club.

He had another problem too – he wanted to go to the toilet. He wasn't desperate yet, but the thought of not being able to go was steadily making it worse. And he couldn't go because he didn't have his glasses and without them he'd never find his way back to the seat. It had happened to him once before; he'd wandered up and down the aisle in the dark until his embarrassed girlfriend had waved to him. And that was the last time he'd dated her.

He shifted uncomfortably in his seat. His arm reached

around her shoulders and she snuggled against him, one of her hands resting on his thigh. The area under her hand became the centre of his feelings until the weight caused stirrings elsewhere. He kissed her cheek softly and then her lips hard as she turned her head towards him, her fingers increasing the pressure on his leg. Well, he'd bided his time for two weeks now so as not to spoil things; maybe now was the time to make his move. His heart thumping, his head filled with concentrated love and the desire to urinate overpowered by a stronger desire, he put his free hand on her wrist and stroked the silky material of her blouse. He drew his trembling and cautious fingers to the centre buttons and poked a finger through an opening, giddy at the feel of the warm flesh of her tummy. After a few moments of making circling motions with his exploratory finger and waiting for the rebuttal, he withdrew it and moved his hand upwards towards her breasts. He found the gentle swelling and cupped it tremblingly. Her restraining hand rested on his and weakly, without conviction, tried to pull it away. Instead he moved it along and slid it inside the opening of her blouse, getting it stuck between the buttons.

He wriggled it loose and undid one of them, hearing her gasp as his hand reached inside again for her.

My first one, he thought. My first proper good-looking bird! After all those fat ones, skinny ones, ones with big noses, ones with big teeth – at last a good-looking one! Ooh, I'm in love. Wait till I tell the boys she lets me have a feel!

His hand crept inside her lacy bra and felt her hard little nipple, squeezing it between his fingers, pressing it as though it were a button.

Suddenly she screamed and leapt to her feet, pulling his arm up with her.

"I didn't mean anything," he began to bluster, his face reddening as people turned to look at them.

"Something bit me!" Vikki cried. "There's something there on the floor! It bit me leg!"

He looked downward but failed to see anything in the dark. He bent down, more to escape the accusing eyes of the cinema crowd than to discover the offending "something."

"There's nothing there," he said miserably.

"There is, there is!" She began to cry, backing away onto the lap of the person sitting next to her. Someone in the next row flicked on a lighter and leaned over the back of his seat with it, holding a small flame towards the floor.

A large dark shape scuttled underneath the seat.

As Vikki screamed, a woman behind in the next row leapt to her feet and screamed also. Then pandemonium broke loose throughout the theatre. People jumped up and kicked out at or leapt away from something at their feet.

"Rats!" a terror-stricken voice echoed around the cinema, the cry being taken up by others equally frightened.

Vikki began to pound her feet hysterically up and down on the floor, as though contact with it would make her more vulnerable to the vermin. Stephen grabbed her shoulders and tried to calm her just as the house-lights came on. Then the terror really took grip as the people saw the horror between the seats. Rats were flowing down the aisles, branching off through the rows of seats, pouring over the tops; leaping onto the panicking crowd. Women and men screamed as they fought each other to get free of seats, blocked in on either side by stumbling bodies. The exit doors became jammed, people falling over one and other in their bids to escape the death behind them. The big cowboy in the film began his final shoot-out with the villains.

Stephen pulled a rat from Vikki's hair and hurled it away from him, his hands torn by the creatures gnashing teeth. He grabbed her arm and pulled her along the row, pushing at the people ahead of him. Inexplicably, the house-lights dimmed and finally faded leaving the confused scene lit only by the light reflected from the huge screen. Something was biting into the boy's leg and he tried to kick it against the back of a seat, but because of lack of space the rat was able to hang on. He bent down to pull it away and his hands were nipped at by another rat. In desperation, he sat on top of a seat back and painfully raised his leg onto the back of the seat in front, lifting the great black rat with it. Vikki ran from him and stumbled over a man in his last death struggles with three rats. She fell heavily, and was immediately engulfed in bristling bodies, her screams unheard amongst the screams of others.

Stephen grabbed the rat's throat with his hands and squeezed with all his strength but still it clung to him. He felt another as it landed on his back and bit into his coat which he quickly shed without thinking, dropping it and the rat into the row behind him. A man in front saw his plight and bravely grabbed at the rat clinging to his leg and pulled. Abruptly, the creature released its grip and turned on the man, biting into his face.

He went down screaming in agony.

The boy looked over the seats and saw there was nothing he could do to save his rescuer. He looked around but seeing no clear line of exit, he jumped up onto the back of a seat and carefully began to walk along the rows, using peoples' shoulders where he could, but mostly depending on luck to keep his balance. He slipped a few times but managed to spring upright again, the fear inside him giving him the extra strength he needed to keep going. The holocaust around him became unreal. It was a nightmare, the strange light from the screen heightening the unearthly effect.

A man in front lifted a rat above his head and threw it away from him, hitting the boy with its long body and causing him to slip between the rows again. He landed heavily on his back and lay there stunned for a few moments. Someone stumbled and fell across him, struggling with something in his arms. The rat was pushed into Stephen's chest causing him to shout out in anguish. He beat at both rodent and man with his fists, cursing and crying at the same time. The weight was lifted from him as the man regained his feet and staggered on, the rat still clinging to his arms, another around his shoulders, chewing at his neck.

The boy got to his feet and climbed onto the seats again, continuing his hazardous journey across the sea of helpless people. Many were in the aisles now, their panic pressing them together in the confined space, preventing the use of speed as a means of escape. The doors were blocked with scrambling bodies and those that managed to get through were being chased into the foyer by the vermin.

An elderly couple near him clung together in a last desperate embrace, the vermin biting at their legs and buttocks, finally bringing them down to their knees.

Another man sat rigid in his seat, eyes still on the screen as though watching the film, hands clenching the seat-arms. A rat sat on his lap gnawing a hole into his stomach.

A group of teenage boys had formed a circle, back to back, and were slowly making their way up the aisle, kicking out at the vermin with their heavy boots. Unfortunately they could get no further than the thronging mass of people around the exit.

The people in the balcony above were no better off; they only had two exits of retreat and rats were pouring through these. They were forced back by the bodies of others and many were toppling over the rail into the theatre below.

Stephen went on, sobbing with fright, and at last reached the front stalls. It was comparatively empty of people and vermin, the sides and the exits of the cinema now being the main points of disorder. He leapt onto the floor and headed towards the stage. He managed to get one leg onto it, quickly finding his feet again. A stream of black, furry bodies emerged from the curtains at one side making straight towards him. He turned to run in the opposite direction but slipped in his own blood from the torn leg. The vermin were on him in an instant, smothering his body with their own foul-smelling forms, biting into him, pushing each other aside to get at his flesh. His arms beat at them growing weaker and weaker at every effort until he finally lay them across his face for protection, allowing the creatures to gorge themselves on his body.

Raising one arm from his eyes, he stared up uncomprehendingly at the huge coloured screen above him. His eyes read the words, and his voice spoke them faintly, but his brain did not understand. He whispered "The End".

George Fox had worked at the zoo for twenty-odd years now. Unlike many of his comrades he had a deep regard for the animals in his care; he worried when one of his lions was unwell, pampered his pet gazelle when it was off its food and once even spent a sleepless night at the side of a dying snake.

When hooligans had broken into his bird-house and for no other reason than sheer bloodlust had slaughtered thirty of his exotically coloured winged friends, he'd broken down and cried for three days. He had a deep sympathy and understanding of his animals, big or small, ferocious or docile. Even when a monkey had bitten off half his ear a few years back he hadn't reprimanded it, but gently put it down, ignoring the pain, and quietly left the cage clasping a blood-soaked handkerchief to his injured part.

And tonight, he felt the zoo was restless. There was a stillness in the air, a quietness unatural to London's large animal estate – but the animals weren't sleeping. As he made his rounds he noticed the beasts prowling to and fro in their cages, the monkeys huddled together staring out nervously into the night, the birds silently blinking on their perches. Only the lunatic laugh of the Hyena disturbed the uneasy silence.

"Easy now, Sara," he soothingly reassured his favourite cheetah in the large cat-house. "Nothing to be nervous of."

Suddenly, the screeching of birds broke through the night. Sounds like the aviary, he told himself, making for the door and running towards the tunnel that led under the public road to the canal where the fantastic bird sanctuary stood. He was joined by another keeper at the entrance of the underground passage.

"What's up, George?" the man gasped.

"Don't know yet, Bill. Something disturbed the birds, sounds like they're going mad."

They plunged into the dark tunnel using their torches for added light. As they emerged on the other side they heard a squeal from the giraffe section. To their horror they saw one of the graceful creatures racing round its enclosure with large black creatures clinging to its trembling body. It plunged into the water acting as a moat around its paddock and thrashed about crazedly.

"Oh my Gawd – what is it?" asked Bill, unsure of what he'd seen in the night light.

"I'll tell you what it is," cried George. "It's those bloody rats. The ones that are supposed to have been exterminated –

the giant rats!" He took several steps towards the helpless animal but then turned back to Bill. "Back to the office, quick. Get on the phone to the police – tell them it's an attack on the zoo by the rats! Tell them we need every available help we can get! Hurry!"

He ran towards the giraffe again, knowing there was nothing he could do for the poor creature, but going on anyway. He turned as he heard a human scream coming from the tunnel and saw Bill emerge, swarming with black shapes and what must have been blood gushing from his head. He saw him go down, half rise and slump forward again.

"God Almighty," he breathed. He had to get to the telephone. There was another ticket office in this section but would mean passing the rat-filled tunnel and crossing the bridge over the canal. And the canal must have been where they came from. Those bastards said they'd cleared out the rats, they were all dead or dying. But the vermin are killing my animals. My poor animals!

He moaned aloud, not knowing what to do. Finally, he decided on a plan of action, trying to ignore the cries from the rat-besieged animals in that section. He ran towards the fence protecting the zoo from the dividing road and scrambled over it in hurried clumsiness. He fell over onto the other side and as he sprawled there he saw the lights of an approaching car. Scrambling to his feet, he ran into the road, waving his arms frantically. At first it seemed as though the car was going to drive on, but the driver must have seen his uniform in the glare of his headlights. It screeched to a halt causing George to jump to one side to avoid being hit.

The excited keeper was shouting instructions even as the driver was winding the window down. At the uncomprehending look on the motorist's face, George began again: "Call the police, tell them rats, hundreds of them, are attacking the zoo. If they don't get here soon, the bastards will slaughter my animals! Move, man, move!"

As the car sped off a horrifying thought struck George. When the police and the soldiers got there, the only weapon they'd be able to use would be gas. And gas would be just as lethal to his animals as it would be to the vermin. He cried out in despair and ran across the road to the main entrance of the zoo. Climbing the turnstile, he saw the figures of two other keepers on night duty approaching him at a run.

"Is that you, George?" one of them shouted, shining a torch into his face.

"Yes, it's me," he answered, shielding his eyes with his arm.

"Get out, George, come on. The whole place is swarming with rats! Those giant ones. They're after the animals."

"No, we've got to let them out, turn them loose – we can't let them be slaughtered."

"Not bloody likely, we're getting out, there's nothing we can do. And you're coming with us!" So saying, he grabbed the old keeper's arm and tried to pull him back towards the turnstile. George struck out blindly, knocking the torch from his colleague's grasp and ran off towards the main office.

"Leave him, Joe," the other man said. "We'll only get ourselves killed chasing him. Let's get out of here."

Reluctantly, the first man shook his head and climbed the turnstile into the street.

George ran, his lungs bursting, ignoring the dark shapes that were streaming from the tunnel, and tore up the short flight of steps that led to the office where all the keys to the cages were kept. By now, the zoo had erupted into an explosion of sound. Roars, shrieks, squawks, bellows – all combined to create tumultuous pandemonium. He snatched as many key bunches from their racks as he could carry, knowing exactly which belonged to each section, and ran from the office.

He stopped aghast at the sight of the mighty gorilla, the old man of the zoo, recapturing its ancient primitive majesty, pulling the rats apart with its great hands, crushing their bones with its immense strength, tossing them away like limp rags. But even its might had to succumb to the unlimited number of razor-toothed vermin. They swarmed over the gorilla, enraged by its strength, and brought it crashing to the floor where it still fought bravely on.

George watched the impressive creatures death-struggle in fascinated silence but movements around his legs brought him to his senses. Looking down, he saw the wretched-looking dark bodies flowing past him, inexplicably ignoring him. In a rage, he kicked out at them, but still they sped on, eager to fill themselves on the trapped animals.

The keeper ran with them, unlocking cages and swinging their doors open wide as he went. Many of the unfortunate animals merely crouched at the rear of their abodes whilst others saw their chance for freedom and hurled themselves through the open doors. The birds were the luckiest -- they could take to the air. But for the other creatures, their only means of escape was speed. The prouder ones stayed to fight and killed many of the vermin before they themselves fell, but the majority chose to flee. When they reached the outer fences of the zoo, they threw themselves at it, going mad with the frustration of being trapped. Some managed to clear it -- the apes or the more fleet-footed -- but the others either cringed against it or raced around its perimeter.

The old keeper found himself at the big cat-house. Still he hadn't been attacked by the vermin; his mind never questioned it, he was too distressed over the plight of his beloved animals to worry about his own safety. The roars were deafening as he ran for the iron cages, the cats snarling both in fear and defiance. He reached the lions and unhesitatingly unlocked the metal doors.

"Come on, Sheik, come on Sheba," he called to them softly, urging them to come out. He raced along, unlocking all the cages, oblivious to the danger. The lion sprang forward with an angry roar as it saw several dark shapes coming through the doors of the cat house. It tore them into shreds, tossing them into the air with its jaws, ripping their bodies with its claws. As more poured in, the other cats joined with the lion in the slaughter of the vermin; the tiger, the leopard, the panther, the puma, the jaguar, and the cougar -- all joined in the fight against the common foe. Only the cheetah remained in its cage.

"Come on now, Sara, you must come out," pleaded George, but the cautious animal merely snarled from the back of the cage, baring its teeth, raising a claw.

"Please, Sara, there's a good girl. There's nothing to be afraid of. You've got to come out." In desperation, he began to scramble into the cage. "Come on, girl, its only old George. I've come to help you."

He slowly advanced on the cheetah, hand outstretched, talking soothingly all the time. The animal crouched away, snarling more ferociously.

"It's me, Sara, George. Only old George."

The cat sprang at the old keeper and within seconds reduced him to a bloodied carcass, dragging the dead body around its cage in triumph.

Then it sprang from the cage and streaked towards the fight between cat and rodent, but instead of attacking the rodents, it leapt upon the back of the panther, sinking its teeth into its shoulder. Still the vermin poured in and the battle between might and multitude continued to its bitter end.

Chapter 16

Harris drove through the clutter of military and police vehicles that jammed Whitehall. He was waved down several times by the police and asked to show his pass. When he did, they briskly waved him on, saluting curtly. He threaded his way through to the granite-grey Ministry of Defence building, now the operations' headquarters. The drive through the deserted streets had been eerie to say the least; the only times he'd experienced anything like it had been in the pre-dawn hours, returning from a late-night celebration, when London's concrete canyons seemed virtually devoid of life and the noises of traffic and people were something unreal, hard even to imagine. But even then, there had usually been the sight of another lonely car or perhaps a man on his bike returning from night work. But today there had been nothing. He hadn't even seen any army scout cars that he knew were patrolling the streets, checking that the city was empty, that no unauthorised person remained. For the past two days, there had been a lot of trouble with looters – scavengers who saw the chance of a lifetime to fill their pockets without hindrance. They had been wrong; security had never been tighter. To be in London now, without authorisation, meant immediate arrest and the whole area was concentrated with police and army personnel with the express task of enforcing the government ban.

"Will it work, darling?" Judy interrupted his thoughts.

He turned towards her, smiling tightly, unable to hide his unease. "It's got to, hasn't it?" he said. Stopping to allow an army lorry to pull out from a row of other brown vehicles all filled with soldiers wearing heavy protective suits and each carrying gas masks balanced on their knees, he reached out and squeezed her hand. As part of the newly reorganised "action committee" he'd been able to use some influence to keep Judy with him instead of being shipped off to the country for five days. Not that he'd wanted her to stay; the danger involved today (and possibly the next couple of days to anyone still in the city could be great. The whole operation was unpredictable to a certain extent. But she'd insisted on staying with him and he had managed to get her dispensation from the ban, having her conscripted into the large administration organisation necessary for "Operation Extirpate."

"Operation Extirpate," as it was named was based on a simple plan put forward by Harris, and the idea that had placed him back on the committee. It was the sort of inspiration that could only have come from someone not used to or bogged down by the intricacies of a scientific mind, so bold and uncomplicated was its concept. After the initial shock of the rats' counter-attack, the members of the original team had sunk into a state of confusion and despair; the vermin had swiftly become immune to the virus although the disease they carried had been considerably weakened. But they, themselves, had become stronger, almost as if they had a burning desire for revenge, and they wreaked havoc, not just in East London, but all over the city, leaving a trail of bloody slaughter wherever they emerged from their lairs. There had been many attacks that fateful Tuesday night; a cinema, a hospital, an old people's home – even a public house. The animals in London zoo had suffered a terribly vicious onslaught, many escaping to the surrounding park and those that couldn't be captured had to be shot. There had been mass individual attacks, people alone having no chance against the overwhelming vermin. Reports had come in throughout the night of destruction and bloodshed.

An emergency meeting was held between the committee and government officials. Foskins didn't attend – he had been dismissed from office by the P.M. instantly the news broke and wasn't seen again in the hectic days that followed. New members were added to the original team but the new plan had been devised before the change had had time to take effect.

When Harris had thought of the idea, he'd blurted it out almost immediately without giving himself time to think. If he had, he reflected later, he would probably have held his tongue with the notion that it was too simple, too broad in concept, and that if it had any merit, then one of the shrewder, more scientific members of the team would have produced it.

The idea, stemming from a previous team meeting, was basically this: as gas was the only proven method of destroying the vermin, they had to be lured into the open for the gas to be effected upon them; this could be achieved by the use of ultrasonic sound beams set up at strategic points all over the city sending out sound-waves to the widest area possible, luring the rats into the open where the gas could be used. To Harris' amazement, the idea was agreed on in principle with only slight reservations; a few refinements to be thrashed out. London would have to be evacuated. It was drastic, but then the consequences would be fatal if the necessary steps were not taken. Londoners would have to leave their homes and migrate to the surrounding countryside if they were to escape the effects of the vast quantity of gas that had to be used. Evacuation was essential anyway to avoid the attacks from the rats. Safety could not be guaranteed any more. Huge enclosures would be built in the parks, as many as possible in the time, and the transmitters placed inside where the high-frequency sound waves would be sent out. The right pitch could easily be found by testing captive black rats. Once inside the enclosures, the entrances would be blocked and the deadly gas poured in. Because of the danger to anyone on the ground, helicopters would be used to hover over the enclosures to drop the gas into them, and ground troops would stand by outside in heavily armoured trucks armed with water-cannons, flame throwers and more gas. The building of the compounds and the complete evacuation of London (save for those people vital to the running of the city's essential services) would have to be achieved within six days at the most – otherwise the risk of the fast multiplying rodents completely overrunning the city would be too great. It was no time to ponder over the very existence of the vermin; their size, their strength, where they'd originated from, how their numbers had grown despite the virus, why they were so much more cunning than the smaller of their species (what gave them the instinct to lie low while the infection was taking effect on their companions). All these questions would have to be answered later. For now it was a question of survival.

That day – the plan had to be created, devised and put into action throughout the night – the city was declared to be in a state of emergency. The inhabitants were informed they were to be evacuated in sections, although thousands left without any urging at all on hearing of the night's events; village halls, churches, schools – all public buildings – were to be used as temporary shelters; huge marquees and tents were to be erected in fields; people were asked to stay with relatives if they had any in other parts of the country; an order was made known that looters would be shot on sight; any unauthorised person found in London after the sixth day would be arrested (it was known that all the people living in the city would never be cleared but at least the emergency laws would keep them indoors and hopefully away from harm).

Mercifully, the area south of the river had not been affected as yet, but it was decided to clear the inner boundaries of the sprawling suburbs as an extra precaution.

Many people protested; they didn't want to leave their homes, *they* weren't afraid of the vermin. But they were given no choice – if they wouldn't leave peacefully, then they were forced, there being no time for politeness or argument. The period of exile would be two weeks from the day of the first gas onslaught. Time would be needed to ensure that every

last rodent was exterminated; the sewers would be completely
and utterly filled with gas; basements, tunnels, ruins – any
possible place that could harbour the vermin would be cleared
and thoroughly cleansed.

Whether the shame and the disgrace in the eyes of the world
would ever be erased was another matter.

The barricades around the parks went up in remarkably
swift time, their use being more to confine the gas in a more
concentrated area than to contain the rats. The roads out of
London were jammed with cars and coaches, and trains ran
non-stop services into the neighbouring provinces. Troops
poured in to patrol the streets and to train for the emergency.
More protective clothing was mass-produced in a very short
time for the police and army. Any public demonstration was
quickly broke up and dealt with, peacefully if possible.

At first, it looked as though the city would never be ready
for the oncoming battle but miraculously – and mostly due
to the cooperation, caused by fear, of the public – on the
fifth day the stage was almost set. Last minute conferences
were held, revisions to existing plans made, final instructions
to helicopter crews and the army given, and then the long vigil
through the empty night, waiting for the dawn and the deciding climax it would bring.

Harris and Judy had laid awake most of the night, making
love, talking – trying to push thoughts of the on-coming
day's events from their minds. They'd finally fallen into fitful
sleep as the grey dawn forced the night darkness aside, the
sun slowly rising upon a strangely still city.

When they awoke, their tiredness evaporated instantly as
thoughts of the day flooded their minds. Judy cooked a breakfast which was left almost untouched and they made ready
to go out into the deserted streets. As they opened their front
door they saw a black rat scurry across the road into the small
square park opposite. They hurried to their car and drove off,
Harris glancing into his rear-view mirror, almost expecting to
see the road behind him filled with vermin.

They finally reached the Ministry of Defence building,
parked beside a shining Rolls Royce, and made their way into
the gloomy entrance showing their passes. On their way down

the endless corridors to their respective operations rooms they encountered a beaming Howard.

"Good morning! All set for the big day?" he clapped his hands together enthusiastically.

"Ready enough," smiled the teacher.

"I've been here all night. Spent a few hours on a camp bed. Everything's set for the big operation."

"Good."

"I'd better get to my room," said Judy. "Locating sewer entrances from those old maps and positioning them on new street maps isn't my idea of fun, but if it all helps the cause . . ."

They all turned at once as a familiar figure came striding towards them from the other end of the corridor, waving his arm at them. As the figure drew nearer they realized with shock that it was Foskins. Tieless, badly in need of a shave, but with an excited look in his eyes.

"Good Lord, what are you doing here?" asked Howard, looking incredulously at the ex-Under-Secretary.

"I've been around since last Tuesday," he said, the excitement giving away to a look of bitterness. He pulled at his open shirt collar and buttoned his jacket. "Before our last, er, unsuccessful operation, I ordered a search through records of anyone entering the country within the past two to three years who'd come from a tropical zone."

"You mean the sort of country that would breed this type of rat – or at least something like it?" said Howard.

"Exactly. But unfortunately, because we thought the virus operation would be so successful, it was rather pushed aside. I – I must admit, I forgot all about it in the excitement that followed."

There was a slightly embarrassed silence which Harris broke: "So?"

"So, after my dismissal, I gathered the information I'd asked for and began sifting through it myself."

"Why?" asked Howard coldly.

"Because, well. . . ."

"Never mind," Harris cut in, glancing at Howard disdainfully. "What did you find?"

"There were many entries from the tropics, of course, but only a few that fit the bill for our purposes. I made enquiries – I still have friends in Civil Service departments – and came up with one man.'

His hand shook as he held up a piece of paper.

"This man. Professor William Bartlett Schiller – zoologist. He'd spent several years in New Guinea and the surrounding islands apparently investigating reports of mutant animals seen by the locals. It seems quite feasible, for an island in that area had been used for a nuclear test and some of the inhabitants had been affected by radiation. Of course, it was all hushed up, but somehow Schiller got wind of it and decided to do some investigating."

"All right," said Howard impatiently. "But what makes you think this professor has anything to do with the rats?"

"Well obviously the fact that he'd been in New Guinea *and* he'd been involved in the study of abnormalities in animals." In his irritation, Foskins almost became the man he'd once been – been in public anyway.

"Added to that," he continued, "he took up residence in London. Near the docks. In a house by a canal."

"The Canal!" Harris exclaimed. "Of course I've been trying to remember. In the beginning, that's where the rats were seen. Keogh saw them. I saw them! Near the old lock-keeper's house. I used to play there when I was a kid but they closed the canal down and the lock-keeper moved on. I bet it was his house the professor took over."

"This is the address," said Foskins, thrusting the piece of paper at him.

"That's it."

"Oh, come now," broke in Howard, "What does it matter how? So this lunatic professor smuggled in one of his mutant species and took it to his home to study...."

"And allowed it to breed...."

"Yes, allowed it to breed. But that knowledge doesn't help matters now; the operation goes on as planned. Maybe later we can investigate ..."

"But why not now?"

"Because, Mr. Foskins, there are too many more important

things to contend with today. Or haven't you heard of 'Operation Extirpate'?"

"Yes, of course I have, but if you're going to root them out ..."

"I've got no more time for this sort of discussion, Mr. Foskins, so if you'll excuse me ..."

"You bloody fool! You soon sank into the background when your last idea didn't work."

"Huh! You were busy taking all the credit for it – I didn't see why you shouldn't take all the blame."

Foskins paled and then his whole body seemed to lose its tauntness.

"Y-yes, you're quite right. I accept the blame – but I implore you, learn by my mistakes."

"It isn't important just now, don't you understand? Good God, man, we can make all the investigations we like after, don't you see, but today, we're going to wipe them out." He turned towards Harris, who had failingly tried to keep from sympathising with the ex-Under-Secretary. "Are you coming, Harris? We've plenty to do."

"Right." He touched Foskins' arm. "It'll be looked into, don't worry." And I'll make sure he at least gets some credit for it, he thought.

They strode off towards the big operations room, leaving Judy standing alone with the distressed man.

All thoughts of Foskins were pushed from their minds as they entered the bustling operations room. In the centre was a huge map of London, with shaded green areas illustrating the parks and dead red lights indicating the positions of the transmitters. When they came into operation, the red lights would come on. The position of the helicopters was shown by yellow arrows and the troop vehicles by blue. The room was crowded with people, most of them having a function, but many were there as onlookers. Harris noticed the Prime Minister discussing last-minute details with the Chief of Staff. One side of the room was devoted to radio and television equipment; the transmitters would be operated from here, instructions sent out to the troops and helicopters, everything monitored by cameras aboard the helicopters and those set up in the streets. The whole event was to be televised nation-wide, and relayed by satellite to other countries. The P.M. felt his presence was vital, not to the operation itself, but to his political career. To be seen at the head of such a vast life-saving exercise such as this – and seen all over the world – was a bonus few other leaders had shared. He disappeared into the adjoining room to be interviewed by the television networks.

Harris had barely begun to study the vast glass map when he saw Judy at the door talking excitedly to an army sergeant whose job it was to prevent intruders, pointing towards him. He went over.

"What's the matter, Jude?"

"Foskins. He's gone off to that house by himself."

"To do what?"

"I don't know. He just said he had to do something - something that would make amends – maybe he could find the nest."

"Oh, Christ. He'll get himself killed!" He went out into the hall, taking Judy by the arm.

"What are you going to do?" she asked anxiously, suspecting what he had in mind.

"I'll have to go after him."

"No. No, please don't, Harris."

"Don't worry, Jude. I'll beat him to the house – he'll have to find his way there, I can go straight to it. At least I can stop him going in."

"But the sound-beams – they're due to start any minute now."

"That's all right. It'll make it safer. The rats will just head straight for the parks."

"You don't know, they might attack you."

"I'll be safe in the car. I've got a gas-mask and a protective suit, remember – standard equipment."

"Please don't."

He held her to him. "I love you, Jude." He kissed her fore-head. "But I'm going."

Chapter 17

Harris drove recklessly, knowing there was no chance of meeting other traffic. He was stopped once by an army scout car and had to waste valuable minutes showing his pass and explaining his mission. The officer in charge regretted not being able to accompany him but he had his own duties to carry out. He wished him luck and waved him on.

As he drove through the city, the office blocks towering over him on either side, the feeling of being utterly alone became almost overpowering. He wanted to turn back, to be amongst people again, to feel the security of numbers, but he forced himself to go on, knowing he had to prevent Foskins from entering the house.

As he reached Aldgate he saw the first of the rodents. They were running along the side of the road, a heavy black stream of bristling bodies. They were joined by others from buildings, flowing into the main stream, jostling and climbing over each others backs.

He turned his head sharply at the sound of crashing glass and saw the front window of a J. Lyons restaurant cave in as rats poured through it. They were all headed in the same direc-

tion and Harris guessed it was towards the park near the
Tower of London where one of the transmitters was located.
On he went, aware of the gradual build-up in the numbers of
the creatures, but all mercifully ignoring the speeding car. As
he turned into Commercial Road he brought the car to a
screeching halt. It seemed as though there was a huge moving
carpet stretching before him – the broad road was wholly
filled with black vermin, creating an undulating cover over the
road.

His heart froze at the sight. They were coming mostly
from a side street and disappearing into another on the opposite side of the main road. The whole dark mass seemed to be
about fifty yards wide, without a single break in its length.
Should he turn back, find another route? Or would other
roads be similarly filled? And how much time would it cost
him to find another way around? Should he drive straight
through them? What if the car stalled and he was trapped in
the middle of the flow? If they attacked, his protective suit
would hardly withstand their onslaught. His instinct told him
to turn around, to get back to the protection of the military,
but as he looked through his rear window he saw other streams
of rats, pouring from streets and buildings, like molten lava
pouring from a volcano, forming tributaries around obstacles
and joining again to form major streams. He realized the way
back would be just as hazardous.

Something landed on his bonnet with a thump causing him
to swing round to the front again. One of the giant rats was
staring at him through the windscreen, its evil face almost
level with his own, the distance between them only two feet,
a thin sheet of glass his only protection.

It gunned him into action. He thrust the gear-lever into first
and revved the engine, slipping the clutch to build up power.
He moved forward, slowly at first, then eased his foot up
gently to gather speed. The rat slithered across the bonnet
trying to retain its grip with its long claws but the smooth
surface of the car soon defeated it and it slid back onto the
road.

Harris kept his foot firmly down on the accelerator, telling
himself it would be just like driving through a flood-washed

road and the trick was to keep going, slowly but steadily. The car reached the edge of the stream and plunged into the surging bodies. It began to bump as it went over them, the crunch of bones and squashed bodies nauseating the teacher who could only force his eyes on the road ahead and will his foot to stay on the pedal. The rats seemed oblivious to the car, making no attempt to escape its crushing wheels. Several leapt across the bonnet and roof -- one jumped at the side window, cracking but not breaking it. Twice the car slid on the wet blood its wheels were soaked in and Harris had to fight to keep it in a straight line, praying he wouldn't stall the engine.

He felt a thump on the roof above his head, then a pointed head appeared at the top of the windscreen, its nose twitching from side to side, the tips of its claws spread flat against the glass.

Harris pushed himself back against his seat in sheer frightened reaction, almost allowing his foot to slip from the accelerator pedal but automatically dipping his clutch to avoid stalling. The creature flopped onto the bonnet, mainly because of the car's jolt, and turned to face the man inside.

It seemed even bigger than the usual giant rat and Harris wondered why it wasn't affected by the sound waves as much as the others. He quickly recovered his wits and drove on, trying to ignore the monster glaring evilly at him through the glass. The sharp squeals of the rats trapped between his tyres strengthened his hate for them and this spurred him on.

Suddenly the rat on the bonnet lunged at the windscreen, baring its teeth and using them to try and shatter the glass. The glass held, but the teacher knew it wouldn't stand up to too much pressure. With relief, he realised he was almost through the black writhing mass and he began to gather speed. The rat lunged again causing a large jagged scratch to appear across the windscreen. At last the car broke through the vermin river and Harris immediately pushed it into second then third gear. He knew he had to shake the monster off quickly before the glass shattered and he began to turn the wheel jerkily from side to side hoping to dislodge his unwelcome passenger.

But he was too late.

The rat took a final desperate lunge at the windscreen almost as though it knew it was its last chance and the whole of Harris vision became cloudy white as the glass shattered into a myriad of tiny cracks.

Harris found himself staring directly into the face of the rat. Its head had broken through and it struggled to enlarge the hole to accommodate the rest of its powerful body. It bared its bloodied incisors at the teacher, its eyes glaring and bulbous because of the restraining glass that pulled its skin back at the neck. Harris knew it would be a matter of seconds before the glass gave and the creature plunged through onto his exposed face. He jammed on the brakes, knowing and fearing what he had to do next. As the car came to a skidding halt he pulled on the heavy gloves of his protective suit and opened the door on his side. He jumped out and ran around to the front of the car, grabbing at the loathesome body and pulling with all his strength. The sudden cold air on his face made him realise how exposed his head and face were and the panic gave him even more speed and strength. He pulled the rat free, the glass cutting into its neck as it thrashed from side to side.

He held it above his head and threw it towards the other side of the car, its weight taking him by surprise and weakening his throw. The rat's body brushed the edge of the bonnet and rolled onto the ground with stunning force but it was on its feet immediately and tearing back underneath the car towards the teacher. Harris moved fast but hadn't expected the rat to come from beneath the car.

As he jumped in and began to pull the door shut he felt an excruciating pain in his leg and he looked down and saw the rat clinging to a spot just above his ankle, the tough material of the suit saving him from serious injury. He tried to shake it off but it clung relentlessly increasing the pressure, trying to climb into the car.

Harris beat at it with his fist but to no avail. Bringing his foot back inside but resting it on the very edge, he grabbed at the door-handle with both hands and slammed the door shut with all his strength. The rat gave out a piercing shriek and loosened the grip on his leg. Its neck was trapped between the door and frame but it still thrashed around wildly, its eyes glazed and its mouth frothing. He pulled the door tighter, slipped a hand through the narrow crack for a firmer grip, and squeezed the life from the rat.

When its struggles ceased, he opened the door just enough for the body to flop onto the ground and quickly closed it tight. He sat there shaking for a few moments, feeling no relief because he knew he had to go on. It was only the sound of the roaring engine that brought him fully to his senses. His foot was resting on the accelerator pedal and because he purposely had not turned the ignition off, the engine was racing madly. He eased his foot off, made the hole in the windscreen larger, and engaged first gear, driving slowly at first then picking up speed as he remembered his mission.

He saw many more of the giant rodents, unhesitatingly driving through them without even reducing speed when they blocked the road. At least the idea of the ultrasonic sound waves seemed to be working, he thought. It had flushed the vermin from their nests. Maybe there was some truth in the story of the Pied Piper of Hamelin after all. Maybe his pipes were tuned in to the rats frequency as well.

He looked up through the side window at the sound of a helicopter. It's up to those boys now, he told himself. And their gas.

He turned off from Commercial Road and drove towards the disused canal, the rats now seeming to diminish in numbers. When he reached the street that ran alongside the old canal, it was deserted of any rodent life at all. He spotted a car halfway down the street and assumed Foskins had beaten him to it. He stopped at the place where he knew the house to be hidden behind a high wall and screened by wild foliage. Foskins must have parked his car and walked back looking for the house. He sat there for a few moments, listening for any sound, reluctant to leave the comparative safety of his vehicle. He reached for the glass-visored helmet and got out of the car. He stood there and looked both ways down and up the street. Carrying the helmet in one hand, ready to don it at the slightest cause, he moved towards the boarded-up gap in the wall where the iron gates had once stood. Two of the heavy boards had been pulled aside leaving a hole large enough for a man to get through.

Harris stuck his head through cautiously and shouted "Foskins! Foskins, are you there?"

Silence. Complete, utterly lonely, silence.

The teacher took one more look up and down the street, put on the helmet, hating the clammy claustrophobia it caused him, and stepped through the hole. He pushed his way through the undergrowth, along the path that had once existed, viewing everything remotely through the glass visor. He reached the old familiar house and stood at its closed front door. Taking off the helmet, he called out again: "Foskins, are you in there?"

He banged on the door but the house remained silent. Hell, I'll have to go in, he thought. At least, if there were any rats, they'll have all cleared out by now.

He peered through the broken window but could see nothing through the gloom, the surrounding trees and undergrowth preventing a lot of the light from penetrating into the interior of the house. Returning to his car, he brought out a torch from the glove compartment then went back to the house. He shone the light through the window and saw nothing but two old mildewed armchairs and a heavy wooden sideboard. He drew back at the stench that wasn't due entirely to the must of age. He tried to open the front-door but it was firmly locked. He then went round towards the back.

What must have been at one time the kitchen overlooked the muddy canal and its door was slightly ajar. He pushed it open gently, its creak the only sound that broke the uneasy silence.

He went in.

The smell that assailed his nostrils was even stronger than before and he quickly replaced his helmet in the hope that it would act as a mask. The kitchen still had crockery in its sink, now dusty with time; cobwebs hung across the windows and from the corners of the small room; ashes, still lying in the fireplace, uncleared from its last fire. Whoever had lived here had left in a hurry.

Harris opened a door and went into a dark hall, switching

on his torch although he was still able to see enough without it. He stopped outside a door that, as a child, when the lock-keeper had let him and his friends visit, he'd never been allowed to enter. Not that there had been any mystery on the other side, but because the lock-keeper had said it was a private room, a room used for rest and reading the Sunday papers. He didn't understand why, but the unknown room presented him with deep apprehension, fear looming up inside his very soul. Nervously he turned the handle and pushed against the door, slowly at first but then swiftly and firmly, letting go so that it crashed against the wall.

It was almost completely dark, the dusty lace curtains across the window no longer allowing light to pass through its fine mesh. He shone the torch around the walls, searching and dreading what he might find. It seemed to have been converted into a study; a round globe stood in one corner, a blackboard in another; on the walls were drawings of animals, bone structures, variations of species; a long bookcase, crammed with huge volumes; a desk piled with maps and drawings.

Harris flashed the light back to the blackboard. The chalk drawing on its surface, faded and difficult to distinguish in the poor light seemed to be of a – he removed his helmet for better vision and moved closer. The thin pointed head, the long body, heavy haunches, slender tail – yes, it was unmistakeably a rat. And yet – it was hard to see in the poor light – there appeared to be something odd about it.

A noise from somewhere downstairs abruptly broke his thoughts.

"Foskins, is that you?" he shouted.

For a moment, there was silence, but then he heard another sound. A faint scuffling noise. He hurried back to the door and called Foskin's name again. Silence and then a dull thump coming, it seemed, from the back of the house. Below.

He edged quietly down the hall, one hand on the wall to steady himself. Opposite the kitchen was another door he hadn't noticed before, but now he remembered it from his childhood. It was the door to the cellar and it wasn't quite closed.

He pushed it wide and shone the torch down the steep flight of stairs but was only able to see a small area at the bottom.

"Foskins?"

He took a tentative step down and almost retched at the nauseating smell. He saw that the bottom of the door had been chewed away. If the zoologist had brought mutant rats into the country, this must have been where he'd kept them, Harris told himself, allowing them to breed – encouraging them. But what had happened to him? Killed by his own monsters? And once he was dead, there would have been nothing to control their rapid growth in numbers. But the cellar must be empty now – the sound-beams would have cleared them out. But what of the rat on his car? It didn't seem affected by them. Perhaps there were others like it. Turn back, or go on?

He'd come this far, it would be an utter waste not to continue his search. He descended the stairs.

As he reached the bottom, he saw there was a faint light shaft coming from some point ahead. He trailed his torch along the ground towards it and discovered many white objects littered around the floor. With a gasp he recognised them as bones – many resembling human bones. If this *had* been a rat's nest, they must have dragged their human victims down here, to gorge themselves in safety, or perhaps to feed their young.

He flashed the torch from side to side and discovered cages set around the room, their meshwork of wire torn away, their bottoms filled with straw and more white objects. He played his beam back towards the small shaft of light and then realized where it came from. It was another torch, the kind kept on key-rings, giving out a weak pinpoint of light, enough to allow a person to find a keyhole in the dark. It was lying next to a body and with dread in his heart, Harris directed his torch over it.

The lifeless eyes of Foskins stared brightly towards the ceiling. He was hard to recognise for his nose had gone and one cheek was flapped open wide, but Harris instinctively knew it was the ex-Under-Secretary. The lower half of his face was covered in blood and there was something moving at his crimson, open throat. A black rat was feeding on him, drinking the red liquid with greedy gulping motions. It stopped as the light was shone fully on it, two evil slanted eyes, yellow and malevolent, glaring directly at the bright torch.

As Harris took an involuntary step back, the broad beam took in the rest of the mutilated corpse. The clothes were in shreds, an arm seemed to be almost torn from the body. On the exposed chest, a hole gaped where the heart had once been. Another rat lay half across the corpse's body, its head buried into the lifeless man's intestines, oblivious in its greed to the presence of another human. In his other hand, Foskins held an axe in a death-grip, its head buried into the skull of another giant rat. Another of the vermin lay dead nearby.

It was as though the whole scene was frozen in Harris's mind, as if his eyes had acted as a camera lens and had snapped the macabre scene into timeless immobility. Although he couldn't have stood there for more than two seconds, it seemed like an age, like a void in time that couldn't be measured in hours or minutes.

Dimly, through his shock, something else registered in his mind. Something lurked in the far corner. Bloated and pale. Indefinable.

The paralysing catalepsy was suddenly broken as the rat at Foskins throat broke loose and leapt towards the light.

Harris stumbled backwards, tripping over bones, landing flat on his back. He lost his grip on the torch and it went skidding along the floor, fortunately not breaking. As he lay there slightly stunned, he realised he was not wearing his protective helmet, and it, too, was lost from his grasp. He felt heavy paws clambering along his body, towards his exposed face. He managed to catch the rat by its throat as it was about to sink its teeth into his flesh. The fetid breath from the creature's jaws, inches from Harris' face, struck even more terror into his mind. The rat appeared to be even larger and heavier than the giant species, similar to the one on his car. He rolled over desperately, his feet kicking out and landing a lucky blow on the head of the other approaching rat

Pushing the pointed head against the ground, he beat at it with his free fist, but the rat's claws raked at his body, pounding in furious rhythm, preventing him from using his weight to pin it down. It snapped at the heavy-gloved hand as it descended again and caught the material between its teeth. Harris felt something land on his back and a sharp pain as his head was yanked back by his hair. He rolled over again, trying to crush the rat on his back but losing grip on the other to do so. The trick worked but he felt his hair tear at the roots as he got to one knee.

The first rat jumped up at his face but he managed to turn his head just in time and felt a searing pain as the razor-like incisors cut along his cheek. With his right hand he helped the rat in its flight with a hard shove at its haunches sending it sailing over his shoulder to crash into one of the scattered cages. He made a move towards the axe he remembered seeing in Foskins dead hand, stretching on all fours, becoming like the creatures he was fighting.

As he reached for the axe, lit by the eerie light from his lost torch, he discovered his hand was bare – exposed to the slashing teeth and claws of the vermin. He almost drew it back towards him, to protect it with his body, but his balance depended on his gloved hand. He stretched his arm again to reach the weapon his life depended on, but sharp teeth clamped down on his hand, shaking it furiously.

With a scream he scrambled to his feet, drawing the hand with him. The rat fell back to the ground, two of his fingers between its jaws.

Incredibly, he felt no pain, his mind too numbed by terror and shock for the message to reach his brain. He staggered towards the door, intent on escape, no longer caring about Foskins, no longer concerned with the defeat of the vermin, only wanting to be free of the nightmare. He was knocked to the ground by one of the rats landing on his shoulder. He fell onto a cage and rolled over behind it, dislodging the rat as he went. The desire to cower, to lie down and die swept through his frenzied mind but with a roar, a scream, a cry of rage – he never knew which – he regained his feet, grabbing for the rat as he did so. He caught it by its hind legs and pulled it off the ground. The other rat had jumped at his thigh and Harris felt it biting through the material of the protective suit. As the blood flowed warmly and freely down his leg, he knew the teeth had penetrated the heavy cloth. It added to his fury, giving him extra strength – not a madman's strength, for his mind was now cool and calculating, ignorant of the pain – but the strength of a man refusing to be beaten by an inferior and loathesome creature.

He twisted his body, dragging the rat in his hands with him, ignoring the one at his thigh. He lifted the struggling creature as high as he could, then swung it against the wall with all his might. The stunned creature emitted a high-pitched squeal, not unlike the scream of a child, but still twisted and turned in his grip. He swung again, this time grunting with satisfaction at the sound of crunching bones as the thin skull hit the concrete. He tossed it away from him, as far as he could, not knowing if it still lived.

Reaching down, he pulled at the rat at his thigh, but now the pain became unbearable. He lifted the writhing body and staggered towards the lifeless figure of Foskins. He sank to his knees, almost passing out with the effort and pain, but managed to crawl desperately on. But he could not endure the pain in his leg much longer. With one final supreme effort, he reached for the corpse and collapsed against it. His weight forced the rat to release him but it immediately launched itself into another attack. Harris rolled on his back, drew his knees up, and kicked out with both feet. The blow sent the rat scuttling across the room, giving him time to get to his knees.

He grabbed for the axe and pulled its head from the dead rat. To his horror, Foskins's hand still held grimly onto the handle. He grasped the wrist with his injured left hand and wrenched the weapon free with his right. Turning sharply, he was just in time to meet the charging black beast, its jaws frothing with blood and foam, its eyes bulging with hate. He brought the axe down to meet its flying attack, the blade clearing right through its pointed skull. It landed in a heap before him, dead already, but twitching violently. He had decapitated it.

Harris sank down, his forehead almost touching the ground but a slithering sound brought him to his senses. Looking up, he saw the other rat, the one he'd tossed from him, the one whose skull he thought he'd fractured against the wall, crawling towards him. It was badly injured, almost dead, but still it found the strength and hate to move towards him, leaving a wet trail of blood in its wake.

He crawled towards it and the rat raised its loathesome head and bared its teeth, a sound like a snarl rising from its throat. Harris realised its back was broken, but still it kept coming, determined to destroy him.

When they were no more than two feet apart he raised himself to his knees, lifting the axe high above his head with both hands. The back haunches of the rat quivered as it tried to summon strength to leap, a feat it could never accomplish. The teacher brought the axe crashing down against the back of its neck, shattering its spine at the top, severing its arteries.

The exhausted teacher collapsed in a heap.

He didn't know how long he'd lain there. It could have been five minutes, it could have been five hours. He removed his gloved hand and examined his watch. It was impossible to judge accurately for he had no time-table of the horrifying events that had preceded his collapse. The pain in his hand was excruciating now, overpowering the throb of his thigh. His whole body ached and his cheek was sticky with blood. A sharp pain brought his good hand to his ear and he discovered with shock his ear-lobe was missing.

"Jesus Christ," he muttered. But he was alive and a lightness filled his whole being. The shots I've had will prevent any disease, he reassured himself. All I need to do is get out of this bloody hole.

He sat up and his hand brushed against the dead Foskins. Poor sod, he thought. He must have put up quite a struggle to kill two of the rats. Well, he discovered the nest all right; this must have been where they originally bred, the home-lair.

A sound made his body stiff. The fear came flooding back. Oh, God, he thought, isn't it over yet? He looked hurriedly round for the axe, found it still buried in the dead body of the rat, and retrieved it with a tug.

The sound was like a whimper, a strange mewing noise. It came from the far corner.

Suddenly, Harris' mind flashed back to the moment he'd discovered Foskins's corpse. The photograph his brain had taken. The pale, bloated image he'd seen in the gloom.

Now there were small scuffling noises.

He crawled desperately for the fallen torch, mercifully still working, but its beam gradually growing dimmer. Am I strong enough to defend myself against another attack?, he asked himself. He doubted it. His intention was to retrieve the torch and then get up the stairs and out into the street as quickly as possible.

But as he reached the torch and no attack came, he became curious. He shone the light in the direction of the noises. Something was there, something white or grey, moving slightly. Two eyes were reflecting back at him. Small eyes. Luminous. He moved slowly towards them.

As he drew nearer, his whole body trembled, repulsed at what he saw. He stopped when he was five feet from it, resisting the urge to run, forcing himself to look.

On the straw before him, tucked into the farthest corner, surrounded by human bones, lay the most obnoxious creature he had ever seen, either in dreams or in life. In some ways, it resembled a rat, a huge rat, bigger, much bigger than the others. Its head was pointed, its body long, though obese, and he could see a long, thick tail curling forward, from behind it. But there the resemblance ended.

Its whole body seemed to pulse spasmodically; it was almost hairless, a few grey threads clinging sparsely; it was completely white, or perhaps grey-pink, impossible to tell in the poor light, and its veins showed through obscenely, throbbing in time with the body movement. It reminded Harris of a huge, dismembered, bloodshot eye. He swallowed hard to stop the rising sickness.

He looked into the sightless eyes. There were no pupils, just yellow, gleaming slits. The head waved from side to side, seemingly sniffing the air, the only way he could locate him. The stench from the creature was foul, putrid – almost poisonous. A shape at the side of its large head puzzled Harris. Resisting his revulsion, he took a step closer, realising the creature was crippled by its own obesity.

The lump was almost as big as the head next to it and it, too, waved to and fro in the air. He peered closer, holding the torch nearer to it and saw what looked like – a mouth!

God! It had two heads!

Harris staggered back with a cry of horror. The second head had no eyes at all, but it had a mouth and stumps of teeth. No ears – but a pointed nose that twitched and sniffed.

The obscene creatures mewing became louder as it thrashed ponderously around in its straw crib. But it was unable to move. It sensed the danger and it knew it was helpless. The giant rats Harris and Foskins had fought had been its guards. Guards to the king. But now they were dead, and it was unprotected. Vulnerable.

With a sob, Harris raised the axe and stumbled towards the monster, frightened but knowing he had to kill it, knowing he couldn't leave it to the authorities, knowing they would keep it alive to study its strangeness, its rarity, knowing he would never sleep peacefully again unless it were dead. And if it were to die – he must be its executioner.

He lunged forward and the sightless creature tried to back away. But its gluttony and reliance on its subject creatures defeated it. It was too heavy, it was too old, it was too helpless.

The body popped like a huge balloon filled with dark red blood. Harris became drenched in the thick, sticky fluid, but he hacked away at the pulsating flesh, in a rage he'd never felt before.

"For the people who've died because of you!" he screamed at the dying creature. "For the good, for the bastards, for the innocent – for the rats like yourself!" He hacked at the heads, killing the two brains that had dominated its fellow creatures.

"And for me! So that I know that filth like you can always be erased!"

He plunged the axe deep into the creatures' sagging back in one final thrust, then he sank to his knees and wept.

Soon he wiped his eyes and got to his feet. Taking one last look at the heap of obscene flesh, he turned and staggered from the cellar glancing at Foskins' body as he passed, feeling drained of emotion.

He wearily climbed the stairs and walked through the kitchen into the open sunlight. He stood at the edge of the canal for a few moments, seeing gas clouds drifting through the bright blue sky, secure in the knowledge that the gas would be fulfilling its deadly purpose. He breathed deeply, trying to lose the pungent cellar odour from his nostrils. He winced at the pain in his hand and examined the stumps of his fingers. His heart suddenly ached for Judy. And for people. He wanted to be back amongst them.

He turned and walked back down the path, his body no longer trembling, warmed by the sun. He stepped through the gap and into the street, climbed tiredly into his car and drove away from the old house.

Epilogue

The rat had been trapped in the basement for five days. It had crawled into a dark corner behind a row of shelves to give birth to its litter and when it had tried to follow the sound that had buzzed through its head, it had found the way blocked by a heavy iron door. The sound had continued for five long days, almost driving the mother-rat and its tiny offspring mad with its incessant, monotonous pitch. But they had found food in abundance in the basement, for the owners had ignored the government warning to leave all doors open so that every building would be cleared. They knew that when the city's population returned from their short exile, food would be scarce for the first few days, and their shop would be ready to cash in on the shortage. The rat and its litter gorged themselves on the food, for the young ones seemed only to need their mother's milk for the first three days then finding greater replenishment in the food around them. They grew larger and sturdier day by day, already dark brown, almost black hairs begining to grow on their bodies. Except for one. Only a few white hairs sprouted on its pink, almost white body. It seemed to dominate the others which brought it food and kept its body warm with their own. A curious lump seemed to be growing on its broad lop-sided shoulder, next to its head.

Patiently, they waited for the people to return.

**Give them
the pleasure of choosing**

Book Tokens can be bought
and exchanged at most
bookshops in Great Britain
and Ireland.